PUSHKIN PRESS

THE NEW SORROWS OF YOUNG W.

'Edgar's voice is reminiscent of Holden Caulfield's, full of naïveté and youthful arrogance, thoughtful and self-aware… a touching and tragic coming-of-age tale'

Publishers Weekly

'Plenzdorf has done his country's literature an immeasurable service'

Frankfurter Allgemeine Zeitung

'A magnificent realisation of teenage angst… a classic of late twentieth century European fiction'

BookTrust

'Blackly comic and slickly irreverent… Pushkin Press deserves praise for giving English readers the chance to discover Plenzdorf's wonderful little novel'

Star Tribune

'Hip-sardonic… a mocking parody of Goethe's romantic epic'

Time

ULRICH PLENZDORF was born in Berlin in 1934, and studied Philosophy and Film in Leipzig. In the early 1970s, he achieved fame with the much acclaimed *The New Sorrows of Young W.*, considered a modern classic of German literature, and taught in classrooms across Germany. From 2004 onwards, Plenzdorf was a guest lecturer at the German Institute of Literature in Leipzig. An award-winning and much celebrated author and dramatist, he died in 2007.

ULRICH PLENZDORF

THE NEW SORROWS OF YOUNG W.

Translated from the German
by Romy Fursland

PUSHKIN PRESS
LONDON

Pushkin Press
71–75 Shelton Street
London WC2H 9JQ

The New Sorrows of Young W. was first published in Germany as
Die neuen Leiden des jungen W. by Suhrkamp Verlag, Frankfurt am Main

First published by Pushkin Press in 2015
This edition first published by Pushkin Press in 2018

1 3 5 7 9 8 6 4 2

ISBN: 978 1 78227 445 2

Typeset by Tetragon, London
Printed and bound by CPI Group (UK) Ltd, Croydon CRO 4VY

www.pushkinpress.com

THE NEW SORROWS OF YOUNG W.

NOTICE IN THE *BERLINER ZEITUNG*,
26TH DECEMBER:

On the evening of 24th December, teenager Edgar W. was found seriously injured in a summer house on the Paradise II allotments in the borough of Lichtenberg. Following inquiries by the People's Police it has emerged that Edgar W., who had been living unregistered for some time in the condemned property, had been using electric current unsafely while tinkering with machinery.

OBITUARY IN THE *BERLINER ZEITUNG*,
30TH DECEMBER:

On 24th December an accident ended the life of our young colleague, Edgar Wibeau.

He had many aspirations left to fulfil!

State-owned enterprise WIK Berlin

Director
Union branch committee
Free German Youth

OBITUARIES IN THE *FRANKFURT AN DER ODER VOLKSWACHT*, 31ST DECEMBER:

To our great shock, the life of our young comrade, Edgar Wibeau, was cut short by a tragic accident. He is not forgotten.

State-owned enterprise
Hydraulik Mittenberg (combine)

Director
Vocational college
Free German Youth

It was with shock and disbelief that I learnt of the death of my beloved son, Edgar Wibeau, in a tragic accident on 24th December.

Else Wibeau

"WHEN DID YOU last see him?"

"In September. End of September. The night before he left."

"Did you not think of getting the police to look for him?"

"You can't blame me for this—you of all people! A man who'd had nothing to do with his son for years, bar the odd postcard!"

"I'm sorry! Wasn't that what you wanted, given my lifestyle choices?!"

"Typical! Ironic as ever! Not going to the police was probably the one thing I did right. And even that turned out to be wrong in the end. But when it first happened I'd just had it up to here with him. He'd put me in an impossible position, at the college and at the factory. The director's son —always the star apprentice and straight-A student—suddenly turning out to be a delinquent! Dropping out of his apprenticeship! Running away from home! I mean!… And then he did start to send word not long after that, fairly regularly. Not to me, God forbid. To his friend Willi. On tapes. The language he used was very strange.

> So grandiose. In the end this Willi let me listen to them—even he was starting to find the whole thing a bit odd. At first he wouldn't tell me where Edgar was: in Berlin, as it turned out. And you couldn't make head nor tail of what was on those tapes. But they did at least let us know Edgar was well and even that he was working, not just loafing around. Later on there was some mention of a girl, but it didn't work out. She married someone else. In all the time he was living *here* he didn't have anything to do with girls. But still, it wasn't a matter for the police!"

Whoah, stop right there! Bollocks I didn't! I had plenty to do with girls, if you want to know the truth. Starting when I was fourteen. Now I can say it. You used to hear all kinds of stuff, but you never knew anything for sure. So in the end I wanted to find out the details for myself—that's just what I was like. Her name was Sylvia. She was about three years older than me. It only took me sixty minutes to talk her round. Which I reckon was pretty good going at that age, especially considering that I didn't even have my full charm back then, or this distinctive chin. I'm not telling you this to show off, guys—I just want to make sure no one gets the wrong idea. A year later Mum enlightened me to the facts of life. She nearly burst a blood vessel. I was that much of an idiot I could've pissed myself laughing, but I didn't—I played the little angel as usual. I think it was a bit harsh of me, really.

"What do you mean he turned out to be a delinquent?"

"He broke his supervisor's toe."

"His toe?"

"He threw a heavy iron plate on his foot—a baseplate. I was completely gobsmacked. I mean!..."

"What—he just threw it, out of the blue?"

"I wasn't there, but my colleague Flemming—he's the supervisor—told me what happened. He's an old hand. Reliable, very experienced. Anyway there he is in the workshop one morning giving out the workpieces, some baseplates that need filing. And the lads are filing away and as he's going round checking the measurements he notices that Willi, the boy next to Edgar, has got a finished plate, only he hasn't filed it himself: it's come off the machine. On the factory floor all the baseplates are machine-made, obviously. And the lad's got hold of this plate and is showing it off—it's not even a millimetre out, of course. So Flemming says to him: That's come off the machine.

Willi: Off what machine?

Flemming: The machine in Plant 2.

Willi: Oh, is there a machine there, sir? I wouldn't know. The last time we were on the factory floor was when we first started our apprenticeship, and back then we still thought those things were egg-laying machines.

And that was Edgar's cue—of course they'd had the whole thing worked out beforehand: So, s'posing there is a machine there. Which there could be. It does make you wonder why we have to keep filing these baseplates down by hand. In our third year of training and everything."

I did say that, it's true. But only on the spur of the moment. We hadn't worked it all out beforehand. We really hadn't. I knew what Willi and the others were planning, but I wanted to stay out of it, as usual.

"Flemming: What did I tell you all when you started here? I told you: Here you have a lump of iron! Once you can make a clock out of it, your training will be complete. Then and only then.

It's a sort of motto of his.

And Edgar: But even back then we knew we didn't actually want to be clockmakers."

I'd been wanting to say that to Flemming for ages. It wasn't just his stupid motto, it was his whole attitude—it was like he was stuck in the Middle Ages. In the era of cottage industry. Up till then I'd always bitten my tongue.

> "And the next thing you know Edgar went and threw this plate on his foot, so hard that it broke his toe. You could have knocked me down with a feather. I didn't want to believe it at first."

All true. Apart from two minor details. First of all I didn't *throw* the plate. I didn't have to. Those plates were heavy enough as it was to break a bloody toe or something, just the sheer weight of them. I only needed to drop it. Which I did. And secondly, I didn't drop it *the next thing you know*—I dropped it after Flemming had fired off one more little remark. He was raving like a madman: You're the last one I would have expected this from, Wiebau!

That's when I lost it. That's when I dropped the plate. Just the sound of it: Edgar Wiebau! It's Edgar Wi*beau*! Not even a complete dimwit says "châtau" instead of "château". I mean, at the end of the day everyone's got the right to be correctly addressed by their correct name. If it doesn't matter to some people that's up to them. But it does matter to me. And this had been going on for years. Mum always just put up with getting called Wiebau. She reckoned people had just got used to it and it wasn't going to kill her and anyway, everything she'd achieved at the factory had been under the name Wiebau. So of course then that was it—both of us got called Wiebau! What's wrong with Wibeau, anyway? If it was Hitler or Himmler or something maybe. Then you *would* have a problem. But Wibeau? It's an old Huguenot name—so what? Still, it was no reason to dump that bloody plate on old Flemming's bloody toe. That was pretty heinous. I realized straight away that no bastard was going to talk about our training any more, only the plate and the toe. Sometimes I just used to get really hot and dizzy all of a sudden and then I'd do things and not be able to remember them afterwards. That was my Huguenot blood—or maybe my blood pressure was too high. Too-high Huguenot blood pressure.

"So you think Edgar was just afraid of the consequences, and that's why he left?"

"Yes. Why else would he leave?"

I'll admit it: I wasn't exactly mad keen to stick around for the aftermath. "What does Young Comrade Edgar Wiebau (!!) have to say in connection with his behaviour towards Foreman Flemming?" If you want to know the truth, guys, I'd rather have chewed off my own arm than parrot some bullshit like: I realize now... In future I will... I hereby undertake to... et cetera et cetera! I didn't agree with self-criticism—in public, I mean. It's degrading, somehow. I don't know if you get me. I think you've got to let people have their pride. Same with that role model stuff. You can't so much as fart without some bastard coming along wanting to know if you have a role model and who it is. Or you get told to write three essays about it in the space of a week. Maybe I do have one, but I don't go round proclaiming it from the rooftops. Once I wrote: my greatest role model is Edgar Wibeau. I want to be like what he's going to be like. Nothing more. Or rather, I *wanted* to write that. I didn't do it in the end, guys. Though the worst that would've happened would be them not giving it a grade. No bloody teacher ever had the balls to give me an F or anything.

"Was there anything else, do you remember?"

"You mean an argument, I take it? No, we never argued. Well, he did have a tantrum and throw himself down the stairs once, because I was going somewhere and wouldn't take him with me. That was when he was five. If *that's* what you mean.

But I suppose I'm still going to get the blame for everything."

Bollocks! No one's to blame here except me. For the record: Edgar Wibeau chucked in his apprenticeship and ran away from home *because he'd been wanting to do it for a long time.* He scraped by as a house painter in Berlin, had some fun, had Charlotte and nearly came up with a great invention, *because he wanted to!*

The fact that I went over the Jordan in the process is a real bummer. But if it makes anyone feel any better, I didn't notice much. Three hundred and eighty volts are no joke, guys. It was very quick. And anyway, we don't really do regrets this side of the Jordan. We here all know what's in store for us. That we stop existing when you stop thinking about us. My chances are probably pretty slim in that department. I was too young.

"My name is Wibeau."

"Nice to meet you. Lindner—Willi Lindner."

Hey, Willi! You were my best mate my whole life, now do me a favour—don't *you* start rooting around in your soul or whatever for guilt and such. Pull yourself together.

"I'm told there are some tapes of Edgar's, ones that he recorded? Do you have them to hand? I mean, could I listen to them? Sometime?"

"Yeah. No problem."

THE TAPES:

to put it briefly / wilhelm / I have made an acquaintance / who is near to my heart—an angel—and yet I cannot tell you / of the depth of her perfection / nor of the reasons for it / suffice to say / that she has captivated me /and all my being—end

no / I am not deceived—I read in her black eyes true solicitude for me and for my fate—I worship her—desires of the flesh all are silenced in her presence—end

enough / wilhelm / her betrothed is here—mercifully I was not there to see her welcome him—it would have torn my heart asunder—end

he wishes me well / and I suspect / that this is lotte's handiwork / for a woman is adroit in such matters and of delicate sensibility / when she can keep the peace between her two admirers / it is ever to her advantage / though it can seldom be accomplished—end what a night that was—wilhelm / I may survive anything now—I shall not see her again—here I sit and gasp for breath / seek to compose myself / await the morning / and at sunrise the horses are

o my friends / why is it that the river of genius so seldom bursts forth / so seldom floods in / in great torrents to stir your wondering souls / dear friends / there are many placid gentlemen who dwell on either bank / whose garden houses / and tulip beds and cabbage patches would be ruined / they know therefore how to avert the threat that looms on the horizon / hampering its course with dams and channels—all this / wilhelm / leaves me mute—I retreat into myself and find a world—end

and it is the fault of all of you / who talked me into taking up the yoke and who extolled at such great length the virtues of activity—activity—I have tendered my resignation—I pray you break the news gently to my mother—end

"Do you understand it?"

"No. Not a word..."

Of course you can't understand it. No one can, I bet. I got it out of this old book, this Reclam paperback—I don't even know what it was called. The flipping title page ended up down the bog at Willi's summer house. The whole thing was written in that mental style.

"Sometimes I think—it might be a code?"

"It makes too much sense to be a code. But it doesn't sound like he made it up either."

"You never knew with Ed. He used to make up all kinds of random stuff. Like entire songs—lyrics *and* tune! There was no instrument he couldn't learn to play in about two days. Or like a week, max. He could make these calculators out of cardboard—they still work now. But most of the time we'd just paint."

"Edgar used to paint? What sort of pictures?"

"A2 size."

"I mean, what sort of subjects? Or are there any I can look at?"

"Nope. He had them all at his. And 'subjects' isn't really the right word for the stuff we painted. It was all abstract. One was called 'Physics'. Then there was 'Chemistry'. And 'Mathematician's Brain'. Only his mum was against it. Wanted Ed to get a 'proper job'. Ed got quite a bit of hassle about it, if you want to know the truth. But what used to annoy him most was the times he found out that she, his mum I mean, had hidden one of the postcards from his progenitor... I mean, from his father... I mean, from you. That used to happen every once in a while. Then he would get massively annoyed."

That's true. That always used to piss me right off. After all there was still such a thing as privacy of the post, and the cards were clearly addressed to me. To Mr Edgar Wibeau, the flipping Huguenot. Even to a complete moron it would've been obvious that I wasn't meant to know anything about my progenitor, the slob that was always boozing and sleeping around. The bogeyman of Mittenberg. With his paintings that nobody understood—which was always the paintings' fault, of course.

"And you think that's why Edgar ran away?"

"I don't know... but anyway, the reason most people think he went, because of that thing with Flemming, that's bullshit. I don't get why he did that either. It wasn't like he was having a hard time. Ed came top in every subject without even needing to work that hard. And before the Flemming thing he always used to keep himself out of trouble. It used to irritate some people. A lot of them called him a mummy's boy. Not to his face, obviously. Ed just put up with it. Or maybe he didn't hear. Like that time with the miniskirts. The hotties—I mean, the girls in our class—would not stop coming to work in miniskirts. They'd all show up at the workshop wearing them, to give the supervisors something to ogle. They'd been told about a million times that it was against the rules. Eventually it pissed us off so much that all of us lads turned up for work one morning in miniskirts. It was pretty immense. Ed stayed out of it. I guess the whole thing was just too stupid for him."

Unfortunately I just didn't have anything against short skirts. You can peel yourself out of bed in the morning feeling barely bloody human, but the minute you spot the first woman out the window you start to feel a bit more lively. Anyway, the way I see it people can wear whatever they want—it doesn't bother me. But that miniskirt prank was still a right laugh. It was the kind of thing I might've come up with myself. I only stayed out of it because I didn't want to cause any trouble for Mum. That was my big mistake—I never wanted to cause her any trouble. In fact, I'd got into the habit of never causing anyone any trouble. Which basically means never allowing yourself to do anything fun. That can start to piss you off after a while, guys. I don't know if you get me. And that's the real reason I decided to go AWOL. I'd just had enough of being paraded around as living proof that you can raise a boy *perfectly* well without a father. That was the idea, you see. One day this stupid thought came to me—what if I just snuffed it one day, black pox or something. I mean, what would I have got out of life? I just couldn't get that thought out of my head.

"If you ask me, Ed left because he wanted to be a painter. That was the reason. It was just a bummer that he got turned down by the art school in Berlin."

"Why was that?"

"Unimaginative, Ed said. No talent. He was pretty pissed off."

No shit! But fact was, my collected works were worth sweet FA. Why did we always paint abstract the whole time?—Because I was that much of an idiot I could never in my life paint anything real, something someone could've recognized, a bloody dog or something. The whole painting thing was a fully ridiculous idea of mine, I reckon. But still, it made quite a hilarious scene, me bowling into this art school and straight into this professor's room and whacking the whole of my collected works down on the desk in front of him, bold as you like.

First of all he asked: How long have you been painting?

Me: Dunno! A long time.

I didn't even look at him while I said it.

Him: Do you have a job?

Me: Not that I know of. What would I want a job for?

That should've been enough to make him turf me out, guys! But the bloke was tough. He stuck with it!

Him: Is it in any kind of order? Which comes last, which comes first?

He meant my little exhibition on his desk.

Me: The early stuff is on the left.

The early stuff! Shit, guys! I was on fire. That was a good one.

Him: How old are you?

The guy was seriously tough!

I mumbled: Nineteen!

I don't know if he believed me.

Him: You've got imagination. There's no doubt about that, none whatsoever, and you can draw, too. If you were to have a job, I'd say draughtsman.

I started packing up my pictures.

Him: I could be wrong. Leave your pieces here for a few days. They always say two or three pairs of eyes are better than one.

I kept packing up. Resolute. More of an unrecognized genius than me never lived.

"But the two of you still decided to stay in Berlin?"

"Ed did—I didn't. I couldn't. But I did encourage him to stay. And it was the right thing to do, in theory. After all, there's no better place than Berlin to go to ground and make a name for yourself. I mean, it's not like I told him, 'you should stay here' or anything. You wouldn't get anywhere with Ed that way. We used to live in Berlin before Dad got transferred here, and we still owned this summer house there. We couldn't get rid of it—apparently they were going to be building on the land any day. I had the key to it just in case. The place was still in quite good nick. We went to check it out and I kept telling him I was anti it. That the roof was kaput. That someone must've nicked the bloody sofa covers. (We'd put all our old furniture in there like you do with those places.) And that the whole thing was due to be knocked down any minute, because of these new builds. Ed got more and more into it. He started unpacking his stuff. Well, I say stuff. All he actually had with him were the pictures, apart from the clothes on his back. His patchwork jacket, the one he sewed himself with copper wire, and his old jeans."

*Ob*viously jeans! Or can any of you imagine a life without jeans? Jeans are the coolest trousers in the world. For jeans I'd happily pass up all that heinous synthetic shit from Jumo that always looks so squeaky-clean. I'd pass up anything for jeans, except for maybe *that thing*. And except for music. I'm not talking about Händelssohn Bacholdy or something here, guys—I'm talking about real music. I didn't have anything against Bacholdy and that lot, but I wouldn't say they exactly got me jumping out of my seat. And I'm talking about real jeans, obviously. There's a whole load of tat out there just pretending to be real jeans. Better no trousers at all than that shit. Real jeans, for example, never have a zip at the front. There is one and only one type of real jeans. Anyone who's a real jeans-wearer will know the type I mean. But that's not to say everyone who wears real jeans is a real jeans-wearer. Most people who wear them don't even have a clue what they're dealing with. It always used to massively do my head in when I saw some twenty-five-year-old codger with jeans on that he'd squeezed over his podgy hips and belted up round his waist. Jeans are hip trousers, and by that I mean trousers that slide off your hips if they're not tight enough and only stay up by friction. For that you obviously can't have fat hips and definitely not a fat arse, because then they won't even do up. Once people hit twenty-five they don't understand that any more. It's like when someone goes round wearing a Communist badge in public and beats his wife at home. The way I see it, jeans are an attitude, not just trousers. I actually used to think sometimes that there was no point getting any older than seventeen or eighteen. After that people just end up getting a job or studying or in the army, and then there's no talking to them any more. At least I've never known anyone who didn't go that way. Do you know what I mean, guys? People get to that age and keep wearing jeans that aren't meant for them any more. It goes back to being cool again when someone's retired and wears jeans with braces over a big belly. Then it's cool. But I never knew anyone like that, apart from Zaremba. Zaremba was cool. He could've worn them if he wanted and it wouldn't have pissed anyone off.

"Ed even wanted me to stay there with him. 'We'll manage!' he said. But that had never been my plan, and anyway I just couldn't do it. Ed could, I couldn't.

So then Ed said: 'When you get back, just tell Mum I'm alive and leave it at that.' That was the last thing I heard him say. Then I left."

You're alright, you know that, Willi? You're a trouper. You can stay just how you are. I approve. If I'd had a will, I would've made you my sole heir. I think maybe I always underestimated you. That was sound, the way you talked me into staying in your shack. But I didn't honestly mean it that you should stay with me. I mean—sort of honestly. We would've had a good time together. But not really truly honestly. When someone's never been really alone in his whole life and he suddenly *does* get the chance to be, maybe he's not always a hundred per cent honest. I hope you didn't realize. Please just forget it if you did. Anyway, after you'd gone I got into a pretty mental mood. First of all I just wanted to go and have a snooze, automatically. This was my moment. It was the moment I first started to realize that from now on I could do whatever I felt like. That no one could lecture me any more. That I didn't even need to wash my hands before eating if I didn't want to. I probably should've eaten something, actually, but I wasn't all that hungry. So the first thing I did was chuck my odds and sods all over the room as unmethodically as possible. The socks ended up on the table. That was my personal highlight. Then I grabbed the microphone, whacked the tape recorder on and launched into one of my private broadcasts: Ladies and Gentlemen! Blokes and Blokesses! Upstanding and low-lying citizens! Chill your beans! Ship your little brothers and sisters off to the cinema! Lock your parents in the dining room! This is your Eddie speaking, Eddie the Indestructible…

I launched into my "Bluejeans" song, the one I'd made up three years before. It got better every year.

Oh, Bluejeans
White Jeans?—No
Black Jeans?—No
Blue Jeans, oh
Oh, Bluejeans, yeah

Oh, Bluejeans
Old Jeans?—No
New Jeans?—No
Blue Jeans, oh
Oh, Bluejeans, yeah

Maybe you can imagine what it sounded like? I used to sing it in this really rich voice—the way *he* sings. Some people reckon *he*'s dead. Bollocks. Satchmo will never die, because jazz will never die. That day I reckon I nailed that song better than ever before. Afterwards I felt like Robinson Crusoe and Satchmo rolled into one. Robinson Satchmo. I was that much of an idiot I plastered my entire collected works all over the wall. That way at least everyone would know, the minute they walked in the door: this is the home of the unrecognized genius Edgar Wibeau. I probably was being a right idiot, guys! But I was just on such a high. I didn't know what to do first. I basically wanted to go straight into town and check out Berlin, all the nightlife and stuff and the Huguenot museum. I probably already mentioned that I was a Huguenot on my dad's side. I was pretty convinced I was going to find traces of the Wibeau family in Berlin. I was that much of an idiot, I think I was hoping they'd turn out to be aristocrats of some kind. Edgar de Wibeau or something. But then I told myself no museum was going to be open at that time. I didn't know where it was, either.

So I did some quick self-analysis and figured out that what I really felt like doing was reading, and that until at least the early hours. Then I wanted to have a snooze till about midday and then go and see what the buzz was like in Berlin. That was pretty much what I wanted to do every day from then on: sleep till midday then live till midnight. I never really perked up till about midday anyway—I'd always been like that. The only problem was, I had no stash. I hope you guys don't think I mean hash and opium and stuff. I had nothing against hash, though I'd never actually done it myself. But I'm that much of an idiot I reckon I would've been idiotic enough to do it, if I could've got hold of any from anywhere. Out of pure curiosity. Me and Old Willi once spent six months collecting banana skins and drying them out. They're meant to be as good as hash, pretty much. It had fuck-all effect on me apart from blocking up my whole entire throat with spit. We lay on the carpet, let the tape recorder run and smoked these banana skins. When nothing happened, I started rolling my eyes and grinning like a loon and talking all kinds of shit as if I was genuinely high. When Old Willi saw that he started doing it as well, but I'm pretty sure he was faking it just as much as me. I've never touched banana skins or any of that shit again since, to be honest. No, what I meant was: I didn't have a stash of reading material. Or did you think I'd schlepped a load of books along with me to Berlin? I hadn't even brought my favourite books. I reckoned I didn't want to be schlepping stuff from the past around with me. And I basically knew those two books off by heart anyway. My theory about books was this: no one human being can ever read all the books in existence, not even all the really good ones. So I concentrated on two. And anyway, I reckon every book actually contains nearly *all* books. I don't know if you get me. What I mean is, to write a book you've got to have read a few thousand others. At least I can't see how you'd manage it otherwise. Let's say three thousand. And each one of those was written by someone who'd read three thousand books themselves. No one knows how many books there are in the world. But by this simple calculation you already get a few billion zillions plus a couple for the road. That's enough, if you ask me. My two favourite books were: *Robinson Crusoe.* I bet you'll have a chuckle about that one. I would've never admitted that in my life. The other was that Salinger one. I got my mitts on it totally by chance. No one had read it before. What I mean is no one had recommended it to me or anything. Good thing too. I would've never even gone near it if they had. My experiences with recommended books were usually pretty grim. I was that much of an idiot I would always think a book someone had recommended to me was stupid, even when it was good. Even now I still shudder to think I might never've got my mitts on that book. That Salinger guy is pretty cool. The way he goes creeping around New York in the wet and can't go home because he's done a runner from this school they wanted to chuck him out of anyway—that always used to really get to me. If I'd've known his address I would've written to him and told him to come over and see us. He must've been exactly the same age as me. Mittenberg was a bit of a backwater compared to New York, obviously, but he would definitely have been able to chill out for a bit if he came to us. And better still, we would've helped him get over his stupid sexual problems. That's probably the only thing I never understood about Salinger. I guess that's easy to say for someone who's never had sexual problems. All I can say to someone who's got those kinds of issues is, he should sort himself out with a girlfriend. It's the only way. I don't mean just any old girl, guys. Never that. But for example when you realize a girl laughs at the same stuff as you. That's always a sure sign. I would've straight away been able to tell Salinger the names of at least two girls in Mittenberg who would've laughed at the same things as him. And if they didn't straight away, we could've got them to.

If I'd wanted I could've hit the sack and read the entire book neat. Same with *Crusoe.* What I mean is, I could read them in my head. That was the method I used at home, on the many occasions when I was trying not to piss off a certain Mrs Wibeau. But I didn't need to worry about that now, after all. I started rummaging all around Willi's shack for something to read. Shit, guys! His 'rents must've suddenly come into money. They'd got the entire old set of furniture from a four-bedroom flat piled up in there—the whole shebang. But not one piffling little book, not even a sheet of newspaper. No paper of any kind. Not even in the dump of a kitchen. A fully furnished house, and not a book in sight. Willi's 'rents must've been super-attached to their books. At that moment I started feeling a bit dodgy. The garden was as dark as a pit. I bashed my head about a million times on this old pump and then some trees before I managed to find the bog. All I basically wanted to do was go for a piss, but as usual the word got round my entire intestines. That was always the trouble with me. It was one of the great sorrows of my existence. My whole life I never managed to keep the two bloody things separate. Whenever I had to take a piss I also had to drop a log, I just couldn't help it. And there was no paper, guys. I was fumbling around like a madman all over the bog. And that's when I got my mitts on this famous book I was telling you about, this paperback. It was too dark to see anything. So first of all I sacrificed the cover, then the title page went, and then the pages at the end which in my experience always have the afterword or something on, which no bastard reads anyway. When I got back into the light I saw that I'd actually done a very accurate job. Before I started reading, I observed a minute's silence. I had after all just divested myself of the last remains of Mittenberg. After two pages I chucked the thing across the room. I'm telling you, guys, you could *not* read that shit. Even with the best will in the world. But five minutes later I had my nose in it again. Either I wanted to read till the early hours or not at all. That's just what I was like. Three hours later I'd finished it.

Guys—I was massively pissed off! The bloke in the book, Werther, his name was—he commits suicide at the end. Just gives up the ghost. Puts a bullet through his bloody head because he can't get the woman he wants, and feels mega-sorry for himself the whole entire time. If he wasn't such a complete loon he would've been able to see that she was just waiting for him to *do* something, this Charlotte girl. I mean, when I'm on my own with a girl and I know no one's going to show up within the next half-hour or so, I'll try *anything*. I might end up getting a slap, but so what? Better that than a missed opportunity. Anyway, slaps only occur two times out of ten, max. That's a fact. And this Werther was alone with her millions of times. In that park, for instance. And what does he do? He sits there like a lemon and just looks on while she goes and marries someone else. And then he tops himself. The bloke was beyond help.

The woman was the only one I really felt sorry for. She got stuck with her jobsworth husband. Werther should've at least thought of that. And also: s'pose there really was no chance of him ever getting anywhere with her. That was still no reason to get all trigger-happy. The guy had a horse! If that'd been me I would've been off into the woods like a shot. They had enough of them back then, woods I mean. And I bet you any money he would've found himself loads of mates. Thomas Müntzer or someone. It just wasn't real, guys. Sheer bollocks. And the style. Hearts and souls and joy and tears all over the shop. I can't believe people ever actually talked like that—even three hundred years ago. The whole thing was made up of all these letters from this loon Werther to his mate back home. It was probably meant to seem super-original or spontaneous or realistic or something. The bloke that wrote it should have a read of Salinger. *That's* real, guys!

All I can tell you is you've got to read it, if you can snaffle it from anywhere. If you happen to see it lying around somewhere just nab the bloody thing and don't give it back! Take it out of the library and never return it. Just tell them you lost it. It'll cost you five marks: so what? Don't be fooled by the title. It's not exactly a zinger, I agree—maybe it's badly translated—but who cares? Or you could watch the film. I mean, I'm not actually sure if there is a film of it or not. It was the same with Robinson. I could see everything super-clearly right before my eyes, every single scene. I don't know if you guys have had that. You see everything as clearly as if you'd seen it in a film, and then it turns out there never was a film at all. But if there isn't a Salinger film already then my advice to any director is seriously just make one. There's no way it wouldn't be a hit. Although I don't know if I would've gone to see it myself. I reckon I would've been too worried that my own film might get messed up. I was never really that into films when I was alive anyway. You would never have found me anywhere near a cinema unless Chaplin or something like that was on—one of those mental bowler-hat films where the pigs in their ridiculous helmets get royally fucked over. Or *To Sir, with Love* with Sidney Poitier, if you know that one? I could've happily watched that film every day. Obviously I'm not talking about those compulsory films we watched for History. You had to go to them. They were on the syllabus. I quite liked going, actually. In one hour you could pick up what you would've otherwise had to spend about a million years rifling through history books for.

I always thought it was a very useful system. I would've liked to talk to one of the blokes who make those kinds of films. I would've told him to keep up the good work. You have to give these people some encouragement, I reckon—they save you a hell of a lot of time. They really do. I did used to know a bloke who worked in films actually—writing the scripts, not directing. I'm pretty sure he didn't write those history films though.

When I told him my opinion on the subject he just smiled. I couldn't get him to see that I meant it seriously. I met him one day when they'd packed a load of us off from college to see this film he'd written the script for. Followed by a conversation with the film-makers. It wasn't just for anyone who wanted to go, though—only the best students, the role models. It was a special honour, because the whole show was during lesson time. And of course, first in line was Edgar Wibeau, that intelligent, civilized, disciplined young man. Our star pupil! And all the other star pupils from the other years, two from each.

The film was set in the present. I don't want to go on about it. I would never've gone to see it of my own accord, or if I had it would only've been because my boys the Modern Soul Band had done the music for it. I suppose they must've wanted to get into the film industry. It was about this bloke who'd done time and had now got out and was wanting to start a new life. Up to then he'd been a bit on the wonk—politically, I mean—and being in the nick hadn't done much to change that. He'd been done for assault, for whacking this old guy who'd pissed him off—something to do with his music being too mental and too loud. Straight after he got out he went into hospital, with jaundice I think—anyway, he wasn't allowed visitors. Not that there was anyone who would've come to visit him. But in the hospital, in the bed across from him, there was this propagandist or whatever it was he was meant to be. He talked like one anyway. When I saw that I knew straight away what was coming. The propagandist bloke was going to bend the guy's ear until he finally saw the light, and then he would miraculously fall into line and conform to society. And that's exactly what happened. He joined this wonderful work brigade with a wonderful brigadier, met this wonderful girl, a student, whose parents were against it at first but then ended up being wonderful as well when they realized what a wonderful young man he'd turned out to be, and at the end he was even allowed to go and join the army. I don't know if any of you have seen this wonderful film, guys? The only thing that interested me about it apart from the music was the hero's brother. He lugged the poor bastard around with him wherever he went, the idea being that the brother was s'posed to conform as well. They spent the entire time searching for this propagandist. It was probably s'posed to be moving or something. The brother let himself be lugged—he even kind of enjoyed all the roaming around, and he was also quite into the wonderful student, and she was into him too. There was one bit where I even thought: he only needs to say the word and he's got her, if he wants. From that moment on I had a much higher opinion of her anyway. So he went along with the whole thing, but that didn't mean he was about to conform. No way. He wanted to be a clown in the circus, and no one could talk him out of it. They said he just wanted to loaf around instead of learning a trade and getting a proper job. A proper job... I'd heard that one before, guys! Obviously one of the reasons he wanted to join the circus was so he could see the world, or a bit of it at least. What was wrong with that? I understood him. I really did. I didn't get what was s'posed to be so bad about it. Most people want to see the world, I reckon. Anyone who says they don't is lying. I used to zone out straight away whenever someone started going on about how there was no reason to ever leave Mittenberg. And this brother basically zoned out as well.

I got more and more interested in the bloke who'd written the script. I was watching him the whole time we were sitting in the staffroom talking about how fantastic we thought the film was and all the stuff we could learn from it. First all the teachers and supervisors told us what we were supposed to learn from it, and then we told them what we'd learnt from it. The man didn't say a word the whole time. He really did look as if this whole scene with us model pupils was boring the absolute shit out of him. After that the film-makers got taken on a tour round all our workshops and stuff. Me and Old Willi seized the opportunity and lobbed ourselves at the writer bloke. We latched onto him and stayed with him at the back. I got the impression he was quite grateful for it at first. Then I told him my actual opinion. I told him a film where people are constantly learning stuff and getting reformed is bound to be boring. That it makes everyone see right from the word go what *they* are s'posed to learn from it, and that no one feels like going to the cinema in the evening and carrying on learning stuff after they've been learning all day and just want to go out and enjoy themselves. He said he'd always thought that himself too but he couldn't have done any different. I told him that in that case my advice was just to leave well alone, that it would be better to make those history films which everyone knows are not meant to be entertaining in the first place. At that point he managed to work his way back over to the other film guys who were having our fantastic training programme explained to them by Flemming. We let him go. I got the feeling he was massively pissed off about something anyway—that day or just in general. I'm just sorry I didn't have his address. Maybe it was in Berlin. If it had been I would've gone to see him, and then he wouldn't have been able to do a runner.

"Is there a Schmidt family in the building?"

"Who is it you're looking for?"

"Mrs Schmidt."

"That's me. You're in luck."

"Yes. My name is Wibeau. Edgar's father."

"How did you find me?"

"It wasn't easy."

"I mean, how did you know about me?"

"From the tapes. Edgar sent some cassette tapes back to Mittenberg, like letters."

"I didn't know anything about that. So there's something about me on these tapes, is there?"

"Not much. Only that your name is Charlotte and that you're married. And that you have black eyes."

Don't stress, Charlie. I didn't tell them anything. Not a word.

"What do you mean, Charlotte? My name isn't Charlotte!"

"I don't know. Why are you crying? Please don't cry."

Come on Charlie, don't cry. Leave it out. There's no need to cry about it. I got the name out of that stupid book.

"I'm sorry! Edgar was an idiot. He was a silly, stubborn idiot. He was beyond help. I'm sorry!"

It's true. I was an idiot. Man, was I an idiot. But don't cry. You guys can't even imagine how much of an idiot I was.

"The reason I came to see you was actually because I thought you might have a picture that Edgar painted."

"Edgar couldn't paint to save his life. It was just another of his ridiculous ideas. Everyone could see it, but he just wouldn't be told. And when you said it to his face, he'd come out with some nonsense no one could make head nor tail of. Probably not even Edgar himself."

I always thought you were at your best like that, Charlie—when you were on a massive rant. But it's not quite true that everyone could immediately see I couldn't paint. I mean, they might've seen I couldn't, but I did an excellent job of pretending I could. That's one of the most effective things in the world, guys. It doesn't matter whether you can do something or not—you just need to be able to pretend you can. Then you're sorted. With painting and art and that kind of stuff, at least. A pair of pliers is only any good if it plies. But a picture or something like that? No bastard really knows if it's any good or not.

"It started the first day I met him. Our kindergarten had a play area next to the allotments with a sandpit, a swing and a see-saw. In summer we'd spend the whole day outside whenever we could. It's all been dug up now. The children always used to make a beeline for the sandpit and the climbing frame in the bushes. The bushes were technically attached to the neighbouring plot, but that more or less belonged to us anyway. The fence had fallen down a long time ago and we hadn't seen anyone on the land for ages. And the whole estate was due for demolition. But suddenly I saw someone coming out of the summer house—a guy, totally unkempt and scruffy-looking. I called the children over to me straight away."

That was me. I hadn't really come to life yet, guys. I'd just peeled myself out of bed and I was like a bloody zombie. I couldn't even open my eyes. I hauled myself over to the bog and then to the pump. But washing with the pump water just wasn't happening, guys. Show me a lake or sea and I could've dived in head first, but the water coming out of that pump would've killed me. Do you know what I mean, guys? I'd basically just woken up too early. Charlie's kids had rudely awakened me with their yelling.

"That was Edgar?"

"That was Edgar. I immediately told the children they weren't allowed to go onto the other plot any more. But you know what kids are like—five minutes later they were nowhere to be seen, so I called them, and then I saw that they'd gone over to see Edgar. He was sitting behind his summer house with his painting equipment and they were all stood round behind him, quiet as mice."

That's true. I was never a massive fan of kids, as it goes. I had nothing against them, but I was never a massive fan. They could get pretty boring after a while, to me anyway—or to men in general. Or has anyone ever heard of a *male* kindergarten teacher? It was just that it always used to massively piss me off the way people automatically assumed you were some kind of degenerate or rampant sex fiend just because you had long hair, or hadn't ironed creases into your trousers, or didn't leap out of bed at five a.m. and fling yourself straight under a stream of cold pump water, or didn't know what wage bracket you were going to be in by the time you were fifty. So I went and fished out my painting stuff and flopped down at the back of my shack and started measuring distances all over the place with my pencil the way painters are s'posed to do. And five minutes later Charlie's kids had all gathered round behind me, the entire crew.

"What was he painting?"

"Well—nothing, really. Lines. The children were wondering the same thing.

Edgar said: 'We'll see. Maybe a tree?'

Straight away they asked: 'What do you mean *maybe*? Don't you know what you're painting?'

Edgar: 'It all depends what's on the cards this morning. And how can you know that before you've started? A painter has to get limbered up, you see, or else the tree he's about to paint will come out all stiff.'

They were enjoying themselves. Edgar was good with children, but he couldn't draw to save his life, that was clear to me straight away. I have a bit of an interest in that sort of thing."

Come on, Charlie! They were enjoying themselves, that's true, but you were the one who came up with that tree gag. I was still sat there thinking: It's always the way—every time you're enjoying yourself, along comes some kindergarten teacher and gives you a serious explanation… and then I turned round and looked at you. I felt like I'd been hit by a bus. I'd underestimated you. You were being fully ironic! I think that was the moment the whole thing began, our whole tug-of-war or whatever it was. Both of us wanted to pull the other one across the line. Charlie wanted to prove to me that I couldn't paint for shit, that I was actually just a big kid and couldn't carry on living like this and needed help. And I wanted to prove to her the exact opposite. That I was an unrecognized genius, that I definitely could carry on living like this, that I didn't need any help, and most of all that I was anything but a kid. Also, I wanted her—right from the start. I wanted to sleep with her, either way, but I also wanted *her*. I don't know if you get me, guys.

"You mean he couldn't draw from life? He couldn't draw things he saw?"

"He couldn't draw full stop. But it was obvious why he made out he could: he wanted everyone to think he was an unrecognized genius. I've just never understood why he was so set on that. It was like an obsession with him. It occurred to me that we could get him to come to the kindergarten and paint one of the walls. It couldn't hurt: the building was going to be knocked down anyway. My boss had nothing against the idea. I didn't think Edgar would bother turning up. But he did. It's just—he was so sneaky! I'm sorry, but he really was sneaky! He shared all the brushes out amongst the children and let them paint alongside him—they were allowed to paint whatever they wanted. I could see straight away what was going to happen. Half an hour later we had the most beautiful fresco on the wall, and Edgar hadn't done a stroke—well, barely."

The whole thing worked out beautifully—I knew it would. I knew it couldn't fail. Kids may be boring but they are shit-hot at painting. I always preferred to look at pictures in a kindergarten than in some old museum. Plus, smearing paint all over walls is one of children's favourite activities. It really is.

The teachers were all over it. They thought it was simply marvellous what their little kiddywinks had done. I liked it as well, as it goes. Kids really are shit-hot at painting. And there was nothing Charlie could do. The others nominated her to bring me some lunch. They'd probably noticed that I was into her. They would've had to be pretty dense not to. I spent the whole time adoring her. I don't mean giving her adoring looks and stuff, guys. Not that. It wasn't like I had a particularly devastating pair of visual organs in my bloody Huguenot skull. I only had piggy little eyes compared to Charlie's dazzlers. But brown. Brown is the zing, guys, seriously.

Back on my kolkhoz, I had what was maybe the best idea of my life. It was a pretty good laugh, at any rate. It was a zinger. I got hold of that book again, the paperback, and I automatically started reading. I had time, and now I had the *idea.* I dived into my room, whacked the tape recorder on and dictated to Willi:

(I got it straight out of the book, including the Wilhelm

thing.) *To put it briefly, Wilhelm, I have made an acquaintance who is near to my heart… An angel… And yet I cannot tell you of the depth of her perfection, nor of the reasons for it—suffice to say that she has captivated me, and all my being. End.*

That's how I first came up with the *idea.* I stuck the tape straight in the post. It was about time I sent word to Willi anyway. It was just a shame I didn't get to see Old Willi keel over. I bet he keeled right over. Had a genuine breakdown. Rolled his eyes and fell off his chair.

"Could I see the mural?"

"I'm afraid not—the building's been knocked down. We're in a new build now. I do have one picture by Edgar. But it's nothing much to look at. It's a silhouette. Honestly—he would not be told. This was the next day. I went round to see him; we wanted to pay him a fee. That was when I thought of asking him to do a picture of me, without help this time. There was no one else there, just the two of us. And what did he do? A silhouette. Anyone can do a silhouette. But while I was in his summer house I got a look at his other pictures. I can't describe them. To me they all just looked totally chaotic. They were probably meant to be abstract. But it was just chaos, honestly. In fact the whole house looked incredibly chaotic. I mean—it wasn't dirty, but it was chaotic and messy like you wouldn't believe."

You're dead right, Charlie. Chaotic and messy and anything else you can think of. At first I felt like I'd been hit by a bus, guys, when I saw Charlie standing there in my shack. Luckily it was the afternoon and I was already reasonably lively. But the thing with the money I cottoned on to straight away. Fee, my arse. That was Charlie's own money, and what's more, she was using it as an excuse to come and see me. For some reason I was preying on her mind.

I acted modest at first. I said: But what for? I didn't even lift a finger!

And Charlie: Well, still—without you overseeing it it would never have come to anything.

Then I told her outright: That's your own money. Fee, my arse!

She had a bright idea: Fine. It is mine. But I'll get it back. My boss just has to approve it first. I thought you could use a bit of money.

I did still have some money, but I definitely could've used a bit more. You can always use a bit of cash, guys. But I still didn't take it. I knew what her offering me money was s'posed to mean. It was s'posed to mean she thought I was a layabout or something. I didn't want to give her the satisfaction. After that she really should have left. Only Charlie wasn't like that. It wasn't her style. She had at least as thick a skull as me. Or head. You should probably say head for a woman.

Also, I kept telling her the whole time that I was massively into her. I mean, I didn't tell her in so many words. I didn't actually say anything at all. But I think she realized. Then she came up with the idea about me doing a picture of her. Just for a laugh, supposedly. Yeah, right! Charlie might've been capable of just about anything, but she was a rubbish actress. She really was. It wasn't in her nature. For about three seconds I stood there like a lemon—and then I had my bright idea about the candle. I sat Charlie down on this old stool, blacked out the windows, pinned a sheet of paper on the wall and started positioning her head against the light. I could just as easily have moved the bloody candle, obviously, but I wasn't stupid. I took her whole chin in my hand and turned her head. Charlie swallowed hard, but she went along with it. I was going for that whole "the artist and his model" vibe. Apparently there isn't anything sexy about that relationship. Bollocks there isn't. I reckon that's just something painters came up with to stop all their models running for the hills. Anyway there was definitely something sexy about it for me, and for Charlie too. But she had no chance. Those eyes of hers were on me the whole time. Those dazzlers. I was about to try and see if I could go all the way. But then I did some quick self-analysis and realized that I didn't actually want to go all the way. I mean—I did want to, just not yet. I don't know if you get me, guys. For the first time ever, I wanted to wait. Plus, I probably would've got a slap. Definitely. At that point I still would've got a slap. So I kept calm and carried on drawing this silhouette. As soon as I'd finished, she piped up: Let me have it! For my fiancé. He's in the army at the moment.

Anyone who thinks I was bothered by the fiancé thing has got it wrong, guys. Being engaged is nowhere near the same thing as being married. Charlie had clearly figured out what was going on, anyway. Hence the fiancé. She was beginning to take me seriously. I'd seen that before. Fiancés always crop up when things start getting serious. Obviously I didn't give her the silhouette. I mumbled something about it still being too rough… not enough life in it yet. As if it would've been possible to put more life into it. If only because her eyes couldn't be in it. And Charlie's eyes were real dazzlers, in case I forgot to mention. I wanted to hold onto it, simple as that. I wanted to varnish it and keep it for myself. That made Charlie pretty angry. She stood up and told me to my face: You can't paint, not properly anyway. It's all just an excuse for something. You're not from Berlin either, anyone can see that. You haven't got a proper job and you don't earn any money painting, that's for sure—I don't know how you *do* earn it. She was on a proper rant!

But I was on the ball too. I thought for a second and fired back the following:

The human race is a monotonous affair. Most people spend the greater part of their time working in order to live, and what little freedom they have left inspires in them such great alarm that they will use any means within their power to be rid of it.

Charlie said nothing. She probably hadn't understood a word. No wonder, with that style. I'd got it out of that book, obviously. I don't know if I already mentioned that I was an expert at remembering bits out of books. It was one of the great sorrows of my existence. Though it did have its advantages—at school, for example. I mean, teachers are always happy when they hear a bit they already know out of a book. I didn't blame them. It meant they didn't need to check if everything was correct like they would if it was your own words. So everyone was happy.

"Am I right in thinking you and he had a falling-out?"

"We didn't fall out. I told him to his face that I thought he was a dosser. I half suspected he might be involved in something dodgy. He had to have been getting money from somewhere. I'm sorry! It was silly of me, obviously. But it really was difficult to work him out."

"And what did he do—Edgar?"

"He did what he always did in situations like that, only this was the first time I encountered it: he talked a load of nonsense. I can't put it any other way. You couldn't even take it in, it was that convoluted. Not completely meaningless, perhaps, but *very* weird. He hadn't made it up himself. I sometimes think it might have been out of the Bible. He did it just to confuse people, that was all."

Maybe I shouldn't have allowed myself that particular little jape with Charlie. Still, the look on her face was worth *dollars*.

Next she asked me: So how old are you anyway, young Edgar?

Young Edgar! That's what she said. And she said it again after that whenever she wanted to make it clear to me that she might as well have been my mother. When she was actually only two years older than me, max. I said: Three thousand seven hundred and sixty-seven, or is it seventy-six? I keep getting it mixed up this year. Then she left. I'll admit it, that question always used to piss me right off. Even from a woman I was into. It always forced you to lie. I mean, no one can help how old they are. And if you're *intellectually* a lot more mature than seventeen you'd be a bit of an idiot to tell people the truth, if you want to be taken seriously. If you want to get into an eighteen film, you don't show up at the cinema and start yelling, "I'm only seventeen!" do you? I went to the cinema quite a bit, as it goes. It was better than being sat at home in front of the TV with Mother Wibeau.

The first thing I did after Charlie had left was reload the tape recorder and report back to Willi:

No, I am not deceived! I read in her black eyes true solicitude for me and for my fate. I worship her. Desires of the flesh all are silenced in her presence. End.

Guys! What a pile of crap! Especially that desires of the flesh thing. But on the other hand, it wasn't all that stupid. I just couldn't get my head round that language. Worship her! I couldn't wait to see what Willi would make of it.

After that I really felt like a bit of music. I whacked on my tape of all the Modern Soul Band's records and started moving. Slowly at first. I knew I had plenty of time. The tape was a good fifty minutes long. I owned nearly everything those boys had ever done. They were shit-hot. I wasn't that great at dancing, not in public anyway. I mean—I was ten times better than anyone else, obviously. But I only really properly got going inside my own four walls. When I went out I always used to get annoyed by the never-ending breaks between the songs. Just as you were starting to get into the swing of it—break. It used to massively piss me off. That music needs to be played completely without breaks—you need two bands, I reckon. Otherwise no one can properly get into the zone. The Negroes know that. Or rather African people. African people is what you should say. The thing was, where were you ever going to find another band like the Modern Soul Band? You had to be glad the boys existed at all. Especially the organist. I reckoned they must've got him from a seminary—a heretic or something. I'd nearly bust my balls trying to get hold of all of those guys' records. They really were off the chain. A quarter of an hour later I was on a massive high, for the second time in not very long. Usually that only happened to me once a year at the most. I was starting to realize that coming to

Berlin had been exactly the right thing for me. Because of Charlie if nothing else. I was on such a high, guys! I don't know if you get me. I would've invited all of you round if I could. I had at least three hundred and sixty minutes' worth of music on those tapes. I reckon I had a real talent for dancing. Edgar Wibeau, the great rhythmist, equally good at beat and soul. I could tap-dance as well. I'd fixed some taps onto a pair of plimsolls. It was amazing, seriously. And if we'd got through all my tapes we would've gone to the *Eisenbahner* or better still the *Große Melodie* where the Modern Soul boys played or SOK or Petrowsky or Old Lenz, depending who was on the bill. There was always something on there on a Monday. Or did you guys think I didn't know where to go in Berlin to find real music? I knew that after a *week*. I don't think there was much in Berlin that I missed out on. It was like I was in a constant stream of music. Maybe you can understand where I was coming from. I'd basically been starved, guys! In Mittenberg there weren't any decent bands, ones that really knew how to play music, for about a two-hundred-mile radius. Old Lenz and Uschi Brüning! When that woman started singing, that was it—I was gone. I reckon she's as good as Ella Fitzgerald or anyone. I would've done anything for her, the way she stood up there with her huge glasses doing her warm-up with the band. The way she communicated with the leader without even looking at him—it must have been transmigration of souls or something. And the way she thanked him with a glance when he let her come in on vocals! It made me want to cry every time. He held her back till she almost couldn't stand it any more, and then he let her come in, and she thanked him with a smile, and it killed me. Maybe it was completely different with Lenz. Still, for me the *Große Melodie* was a kind of paradise. It was heaven. I don't think I lived on much more than music and milk back then.

At first, my one problem with the *Große Melodie* was the fact that I didn't have long hair. I stood out like a bloody sore thumb. Back in Mittenberg, being the model child that I was, I obviously wasn't even allowed to have a moptop, let alone long hair. I don't know if you guys can imagine what a great sorrow that was in my life. I used to cringe when I saw everyone else with their manes—inwardly, obviously. Outwardly I always used to say I didn't see what was so great about having long hair if everyone had it, because it didn't take any guts then. Although saying that, people did get given shit about their hair constantly. The minute they started a job. Have you ever had that experience, guys? That face they make when they politely inform you that long hair is not permitted in the workshop or wherever, for health and safety reasons. Or that you have to wear head protection—a hairnet like the ones women wear—which makes you look like you've been branded, like you're being punished. I don't think you guys can even imagine how much of a kick a guy like Flemming got out of that. Most people opted for the headgear, obviously, and took it off whenever they could. Which immediately brought Flemming rampaging into the workshop. He had nothing against long hair, but in the workshop… un*fort*unately… et cetera et cetera. The way he smirked while he was saying it always used to make me see red. I don't know what you call it when people are constantly getting hassled for having long hair. I'd like to know what harm it does to anyone? I always thought Flemming was a real bastard on those occasions. Especially when he went on to say: Just look at Edgar. He always looks well turned out. Well turned out!

Someone once told me the story of this guy—another model child, straight As, very good family—the only thing was, he didn't have any friends. And around where he lived there was this gang that used to tip over park benches and smash windows and that kind of stuff. No bastard could catch them. Their leader was well on the ball. But one fine-ish day they did it. They caught him.

The bloke had hair down to his shoulders—typical! Only it turned out to be a wig, and it had actually been this wonderful model child all along. One day he'd just had enough, and gone out and got himself a wig.

When I first started living in Berlin I often thought about trying to get hold of a wig myself, to wear to the *Große Melodie*. The thing was that, a) wigs don't grow on trees, and b) my hair grew freakishly quickly. About two centimetres a day, believe it or not. For a long time that was one of the great sorrows of my existence. I spent literally my entire life at the barber's. But it did mean that after two weeks I'd already managed to sprout a pretty decent moptop.

"And you saw him more often after that?"

"It was unavoidable. We were pretty much next-door neighbours, after all. And after the thing with the mural the children just would not leave him alone! What was I supposed to do? He was good with children, which is something you don't often see in men, I mean boys. And I think children can always tell whether someone likes them or not."

It's true. Charlie's kids were beyond help. That's always the way with kids. Give them an inch and they take a mile. I knew that. They probably think you're having fun or something. But still, I went along with it with the patience of an ox. Firstly because Charlie reckoned I was great with children—that I loved hanging out with them or something. I didn't want to disillusion her. Me, great with children! And secondly because the kids were my only chance of staying close to Charlie. Try as I might I could never get her to venture onto my kolkhoz again, and definitely not into the shack. She knew why, and so did I. So I hung around that playground day after day. I spun the roundabout or whatever that thing is with the four beams, and I pretended to be a Red Indian. That was how I eventually figured out a way to get them off your back if you want to. At least for ten minutes. I split them into two groups and let them have a battle.

Around that time I got my first reply from Willi. Good old Willi. It'd been too much for him. He couldn't hack it. On the tape were the following words: *Hey, Eddie! I don't get it. Give me the new code. Which book, which page, which line? End. What's going on with variant three?*

Give me the new code! That killed me. It'd been too much for him. It hadn't been completely fair of me either, I'll admit. We did usually communicate using code words. But this had just been too much. A new code. I was kicking myself. When we were in the mood we could bounce stupid proverbs off each other for hours: Yes, well, a loaf always has two ends.—That's as may be. But he who does not dry the dishes, ever shall he eat soggy dinners.—He who laughs last probably doesn't get the joke.—Working all day keeps wet feet at bay. That kind of thing. But *this* had been too much for Old Willi. You should've heard his voice, guys. He was fully bamboozled. What he meant by "variant three" was whether I was working or anything. He probably thought I was wasting away from hunger. Just like Charlie. She was always going on about that.

I had nothing against work. My opinion on it was: when I'm working I'm working, and when I'm chilling I'm chilling. Or did I not deserve a holiday? But don't think I was planning to sit around on my kolkhoz for ever or anything. That might seem OK at first. But any halfway intelligent person knows how long for. Basically until you go nuts, guys. If the only thing you ever see is your own ugly mug it's guaranteed to drive you nuts after a while. The zing goes out of it and stuff. It just stops being a laugh. For stuff to be a laugh you need mates, and to find mates you need a job. I did, anyway. It was just that I hadn't reached the going-nuts stage yet. For the time being it was still zinging. And anyway, I didn't have time for a job. I had to stick at it with Charlie. I was pretty into Charlie, in case I forgot to mention. In a situation like that you have to stick at it. I can still picture me sitting next to her in that playground, with the kids playing all around us. Charlie doing crochet. An idyll, guys. The only thing missing was me lying with my head on her lap. I wasn't shy about stuff like that, and I had managed it once—the feeling on the back of my head had been pretty nice. Seriously. But ever since that day, she'd brought crocheting stuff with her and fiddled around with it on her lap the whole time. She used to come out in the afternoon with the kids, sit down and get her crocheting stuff out. I always made sure I was there before her. Charlie had this way of sitting down that could practically drive you nuts. She must have only owned billowy skirts, and before she sat down she used to take hold of the hem at the back, lift it up and sit down on her knickers. She was very precise about it. That's why I always got there first. I didn't want to miss it. And I always made sure the bench was dry. I don't know if she noticed that. But she did know for a fact that I used to watch when she sat down—no one can convince me otherwise. It's always the way. They know you're watching, and they do it anyway. But it was also worth seeing just for the way she kept her dazzlers lowered every time she did it. The rest of the time she always used to look you straight in the eye. But in that moment she kept her dazzlers lowered. I think Charlie had a bit of a squint. That's why you got the feeling she was always looking straight at you. You know those portraits of people that hang on the wall and constantly look at you wherever you are in the room? Painters have this trick where they just paint the eyes so the optical axes run exactly parallel to each other, which never actually happens in real life. It's well known that true parallels don't exist. I'm not saying I didn't like it. It wasn't that. It was just that you could never tell, was she taking you seriously or was she laughing at you? It could drive you pretty nuts.

I probably already mentioned that I was basically part of the furniture at that kindergarten. A sort of subbie caretaker or something. Practically the only thing I hadn't done was paint the fence. Toy repairs and roundabout-pushing were all part of the service. And blowing up balloons. This one day—it must've been a kids' party—I'd already blown up about two to the power of six balloons and then when I got to two to the power of seven everything went black and I keeled over. I keeled right over. I could stay underwater for four minutes, not eat for three days or not listen to music for half a day (real music I mean), but *that* made me keel over. When I surfaced again I was lying in Charlie's lap. I realized that straight away. She'd undone my shirt and was massaging my chest. I pressed my head into her belly and stayed still. Unfortunately, I'm insanely ticklish. So I had to sit up. The kids were standing around us. Charlie had gone pale. Almost straight away she went off on one: You know what, if I was hungry I'd eat something!

I said: It's just from blowing up the balloons.

Charlie: If I didn't have anything to eat I'd buy myself something.

I grinned. I knew exactly why she'd gone off on one like that. It was because she was massively glad I was still alive. Any halfway intelligent person could've seen that. She was genuinely eating me up with her dazzlers, guys. It killed me. I would've just liked to have sent the kids packing.

Charlie: If I didn't have any money I'd get a job.

I said: He who does not eat, neither shall he work.

I used to find it pretty witty to flip things around like that. Then I stood up, zipped over to my kolkhoz (I made it in two strides) and yoinked up the first lettuce I could lay my mitts on. I don't think I mentioned that for a laugh one day I'd got hold of all the packets of seeds that were still lying around in Willi's shack and sprinkled them all over the garden. The first thing to sprout was lettuce. Lettuce and radishes. I proceeded to wrap my laughing gear around the lettuce. The sand was a bit crunchy, but I just wanted to rattle off the following:

Happy am I indeed that my heart can feel the simple, innocent pleasure of the man who brings to his table a cabbage grown by his own hand.

Obviously I'd got it from Old Werther! That day I think I was the charmingest I'd ever been.

Charlie just said: You nutcase!

She'd never said that before. She'd always gone off the deep end whenever I'd come out with that Werther stuff. I wanted to seize my opportunity straight away and get my head on her lap again, and it definitely would've worked if that stupid Werther book hadn't managed to fall out of my shirt at that precise moment. I'd got into the habit of always carrying it around in there—even I wasn't sure why.

Charlie got hold of it straight away. She flicked through without reading. I stood there like a bit of a lemon. I would've felt like a right idiot if she'd figured it all out. She asked what it was. I mumbled: Bog roll. A second later I'd grabbed it back off her. I tucked it away. I reckon my hand was shaking a little bit. From that day onwards I always left it in the shack, guys. After that I wanted to crack on with the charm offensive and stuff, but then the boss of the kindergarten came charging out into the playground. At first I thought she had a problem with my esteemed presence. But she didn't even see me. She just looked at Charlie, in kind of a weird way.

She said: Knock off for today. I'll take over for you.

Charlie had no idea what she was on about.

The boss: Dieter's here.

Charlie went as white as a sheet, then bright red. Then she looked at me like I was a felon or something, and then she took off.

I was at a loss.

The boss explained: Dieter is her fiancé.

He'd arrived back from the army that day, honourable discharge and all that. I wondered how Charlie could've not known about it. After all they write to you and tell you these things. And then I remembered that felon look. It was s'posed to be *my* fault, *me*, Edgar Wibeau, the dosser, the sham painter, the nutcase! I was apparently to blame for the fact that she hadn't been there to meet her Dieter at the station with flowers and everything. I felt like I'd been kicked by a horse, guys. I think I already mentioned that I wasn't lacking in the charm department. That I seemed to appeal to women, or the female of the species. I mean intellectually or whatever you want to call it. Sylvia had been nearly three years older than me, but I wouldn't have called her a woman. I don't know if you get me. Sylvia was way below my level. It didn't mean I had anything against her, but she was way below my level. Charlie was the first real woman I'd ever had anything to do with. I hadn't expected to fall for her *quite* so quickly. It was killing me, guys. It really was. I think it was because I'd been hanging around her so much. I legged it back to my shack—or rather, I wanted to. But first I caught sight of Dieter. He'd come out to meet Charlie. He was wearing a shirt and tie and holding a suitcase, one of those stupid document cases, an air rifle in a holster and a bunch of flowers; about twenty-five years old, by my guess. Dieter I mean, not the flowers. That would mean he must've served in the army for quite a while. He'd probably made it to general or something. I waited to see if they kissed. But they didn't, not that I could see.

Back in my shack, I made a beeline for the microphone. Old Willi needed to hear about this. It only took me a second to find the appropriate bit:

Enough, Wilhelm. Her betrothed is here!… Mercifully I was not there to see her welcome him! It would have torn my heart asunder. End.

"If he didn't get anywhere with the painting then how exactly was he making a living, I wonder?"

"I suppose he might have been working as a labourer somewhere. But I'm sure we would have noticed that—my husband and I. Or fiancé, I should say: we weren't married at that point. We'd known each other quite a while, since we were children. And then he'd spent a long time in the army. I brought him and Edgar together. Dieter—my husband—had recently been put in charge of barracks duties. I don't know if that means anything to you? Anyway, it brought him into contact with a lot of boys of Edgar's age. I thought he might be a good influence on Edgar. And they did get on very well together. We once went round to see Edgar, and he sometimes came to ours. But Edgar was beyond help. He was just beyond help. Dieter really did have the patience of a saint with him—too much patience maybe, I don't know. But Edgar was just beyond help."

It's true. They both turned up at my shack. Now that she had her Dieter by her side Charlie was prepared to venture into my shack again. She hadn't been in the playground for a few days. Her kids had, but not her. Then she showed up at mine with Dieter. She called me "young Edgar". I knew what that was all about. She wanted to make it clear to Dieter that she viewed me as a harmless nutcase. I immediately put my dukes up. Not actually, I mean. Inwardly. I don't think I mentioned that I'd been in the boxing club from the age of fourteen. Apart from Old Willi that was maybe the best thing about Mittenberg. Of course, I didn't know what kind of an opponent Dieter was. My first impression was that he was probably pretty feeble. But I'd learnt that you should never judge an opponent on first impressions. The thing was, I immediately felt that he wasn't the right man for Charlie. He could've been her father. Not literally, I mean—he wasn't old enough—but in every other way. The way he carried himself was at least as stately as Bismarck or someone like that. He stationed himself in front of my collected works. They were probably the main reason Charlie had dragged him along. She still hadn't quite ruled out the possibility that I might be an unrecognized genius after all. And apart from that, she stuck close to him the whole time. I still had my dukes up. Dieter took his sweet time—I started to think he wasn't going to say anything at all. But that was just Dieter's way. I don't think he ever uttered a single bloody word he hadn't already analysed three times, if not more. And then he was off: I should say it wouldn't do him any harm to focus more on real life in future—on the lives of construction workers, for example. He has them right outside his front door here, after all. And also, of course, in this discipline as in any other, there are certain rules which he simply must observe: perspective, proportion, foreground, background.

That was it. I looked at Charlie. I looked at the man. I was close to effing and blinding. The man was being serious—totally serious. At first I thought he was being ironic. But he was being serious, guys!

I could've kept knocking him round the ring for a bit longer, but I decided to go straight in with my most powerful weapon. I thought for a second and then launched the following missile:

A great deal may be said in favour of rules—much the same as what may be said in praise of bourgeois society. A person who conforms in every respect to the rules will never produce anything tasteless or bad, just as a person whose behaviour is shaped by laws and decorum can never be an intolerable neighbour nor an outright villain; yet say what you will, rules destroy the true feeling of Nature and its true expression!

He came up with some pretty useful shit, did Old Werther. Straight away I realized I could put my dukes down. The man had no chance. Charlie must've told him to be prepared for all sorts, but *this* had been too much for him. He tried to act like he was dealing with some kind of mental patient who was not to be provoked under any circumstances. But that didn't fool me. Any trainer with any sense would've thrown in the towel. Technical knockout. And Charlie did look like she wanted to leave. But Dieter wasn't done yet. He continued: On the other hand, his pictures are very original, and decorative too.

I don't know what made him say that. He probably thought *he'd* KO'd *me*, and now he was trying to soften the blow! Poor bastard! I felt sorry for the man. I let him go. The stupid thing was that just then he caught sight of the silhouette I'd done of Charlie that time. Charlie said immediately: It was meant to be for you, only he never gave it to me. Because it wasn't finished, he said. Though he hasn't actually done anything *to* it since then.

And Dieter went: Well, I've got you in the flesh now.

Guys! That was probably s'posed to be charming. He was a real charmfest, was dear Dieter.

Then they vacated the area. Charlie was glued to him the whole time. Not literally, I mean. With her dazzlers. Just so I would see. But it ran off me like water. Don't think I had anything against Dieter because he'd been in the army. I had nothing against the army. Although I *was* a pacifist, especially when I thought about those compulsory eighteen months. Then I was an excellent pacifist. Just as long as I didn't look at any pictures of

Vietnam and that. That used to make me see red. If someone had asked me at one of those moments, I would've signed up as a soldier for life. Seriously.

About Dieter, I just want to add that he probably was a perfectly OK guy. Not everyone could be as much of an idiot as me, after all. He probably was actually exactly the right man for Charlie. But there was no point in thinking about that. All I can tell you, guys, if you're ever in a situation like that, is don't start thinking about it. When you go up against an opponent you can't start thinking about what a nice bloke he is and stuff. That'll get you nowhere.

I grabbed the microphone and gave Willi an update:

He wishes me well, and I suspect that this is Lotte's handiwork... for a woman is adroit in such matters and of delicate sensibility; when she can keep the peace between her two admirers, it is ever to her advantage, though it can seldom be accomplished. End.

I was starting to get quite into Old Werther, but I had to go after the two of them. I knew you've got to stick at it, guys. You might have won the first round, but you've still got to stick at it and not let up on your opponent. I scooted along after them and muscled in. "I'll see you home," that kind of thing. Charlie was hanging onto Dieter's arm. She offered me her other arm pretty much straight away. It practically killed me. And it immediately made me think of Old Werther. That guy knew his onions. Dieter didn't say a word.

We ended up at Dieter's flat. It was in a pre-war building—one room and a kitchen. It was the tidiest room you could ever possibly imagine. Mother Wibeau would've got a kick out of it. It was about as cosy as the waiting room at Mittenberg station. Except that that at least was never tidy. *That* I could deal with. I don't know if you guys have ever seen one of these rooms that always look like they're only lived in two days a year and even then it's by the head hygiene inspector? And the best thing was that Charlie suddenly had exactly the same thought. She said: It's all going to be different round here. Once we're married. Right?

I set off on a sort of room inspection. First of all I had a look at the pictures he had up. One of them was this crappy print of Old Gogh's sunflowers. I had nothing against Old Gogh and his sunflowers. But when you start to come across the same picture hanging on the wall of every bloody bog in the world, that always used to massively irritate me. At best I'd end up feeling mega-sorry for the picture. But mostly I just couldn't bear to look at it ever again for the rest of my life. The other one was in a clip frame. I don't want to say any more about it. Anyone who's seen it knows which one I'm talking about. It is actually vomit-inducing. Seriously. This wonderful couple sitting there on the beach. Even just the fact that it was in a clip frame. If I want to look at all the pictures in the world, I'll go to a museum. Or a picture might really get under my skin, and then I'll hang it in three different places in the room so I can see it from every angle. But whenever I saw a clip frame it always made me think those people had committed themselves to viewing twelve different pictures a year.

Suddenly Charlie said: The pictures are from back when we were at school.

And that was without me even opening my *mouth*. I hadn't groaned or rolled my eyes or anything. I looked around for Dieter. I'm telling you—the man was in his corner, his fists were down, and he wasn't moving. Maybe he hadn't realized that the second round was well under way. Charlie was apologizing for him all over the place, and he wasn't moving. At least *I* knew what I had to do, guys. My next target was his books. He had shitloads of them. All behind glass. All arranged in order of size. I went into a slump. Whenever I saw something like that I went into a slump. I've probably already mentioned my opinions on books. I don't know what all those books of Dieter's were—blatantly all the Good ones. Marx, Engels,

Lenin. By the shelfload. I had nothing against Lenin and those guys. And I had nothing against Communism and that—the idea of ending exploitation across the globe. I wasn't against that. But I was against everything else. Arranging books in order of size, for example. Most people are like that. They have nothing against Communism. No halfway intelligent person can have anything against Communism. But they're against the other stuff. You don't need to be brave to be in favour of it, and everyone wants to be brave. So they're against it. That's just how it is. Charlie said: Dieter's going to be doing German Studies. He's got a lot of catching up to do. Other people who weren't in the army so long are already lecturers by now.

I looked at Dieter. At this point, if I was him, I definitely wouldn't have left it any longer to spring into action. But he still hadn't put his dukes up. What a fantastic situation. I was starting to realize that if I carried on the way I was going and if Charlie didn't stop apologizing for him, things were really going to kick off.

The only other thing in the whole room was Dieter's air rifle, a hinged-barrel one. He'd hung it up above the bed. I casually took it down, without asking, and started pissing about with it. I aimed the barrel at the couple on the beach, at Dieter, at Charlie. When I got to Charlie

Dieter finally got his arse in gear. He came over to me and pushed the barrel aside.

Loaded? I asked.

Dieter: No, but even so. Too much damage has been done already.

It used to do my head in when people came out with those wise-old-grandpa sayings. I didn't say anything though. I just held the barrel to my head and pulled the trigger. That perked him up at last: That thing is not a toy! Even *you* must have the sense to see that!

And he snatched the gun out of my hand.

I immediately hit him with my most powerful weapon, Old Werther:

My friend… a man is human, and what little sense he may have is to little or no avail when passions rage and he is constrained by the bounds of humanity. Rather—But more of this another time.

The bounds of humanity—Old Werther wouldn't settle for anything less. But I'd hit Dieter hard. He made the mistake of thinking about it. Charlie wasn't even listening any more. But Dieter made the mistake of thinking about it. I basically could've left at that point. Then Charlie piped up: I'll make us a little something to eat, shall I?

And Dieter: If you like! But I've got things to do.

He was off. He planted himself at his desk. With his back to us.

Charlie: He's got his entrance exams in three days.

Charlie must've been having a bad day. She couldn't leave it alone. I was still standing around. And that was when Dieter lost it. He said frostily: You can tell him some more about me *on the way*.

Charlie went pale. It was obvious we were both being chucked out. I'd put her in a bitch of a situation and I was that much of an idiot that I still felt chuffed. Charlie had gone pale and like an idiot I stood there feeling chuffed. Then I left. Charlie came after me. Out in the street I managed to get an arm round her shoulders.

Charlie immediately punched me in the ribs and hissed: Are you insane?

Then she ran off. She ran off, but I went into a completely mental mood. Even though I was gradually starting to realize that I wasn't getting anywhere with Charlie, for some reason I was still on a massive high. At least, I suddenly found myself standing outside my shack holding a tape from Old Willi. Meaning I must have been to the post office. I don't know if you've ever had that, guys?

Dear Edgar. I don't know where you are. But if you want to come back now, the key's under the mat. I won't ask any questions.

And from now on you can stay out as late as you want. And if you want to finish off your apprenticeship at a different factory that's fine too. The main thing is that you're working and not loafing around.

I felt like I'd been kicked by a horse. It was Mother Wibeau.

Then came Willi: *Hey, Eddie. I just* could not *get rid of your mum. Sorry. She's really down. She even wanted to give me some money to give to you. Maybe you getting a job wouldn't be that bad an idea. Just think of van Gogh and those guys. All the stuff they had to do so they could be painters. End.*

As I listened, I knew immediately which bit of Old Werther fitted the bill:

What a night that was! Wilhelm! I may survive anything now. I shall not see her again!... Here I sit and gasp for breath, seek to compose myself, await the morning, and at sunrise the horses are...

Annoyingly that was the end of the tape, and I didn't have any more in reserve. I would've had to tape over some music and I didn't want to do that. And I didn't want to go out and get a new tape either. I did some quick self-analysis and realized that the whole kolkhoz and stuff had lost its zing. I wasn't thinking of going back to Mittenberg—not that. But it had just lost its zing.

"But at some point Edgar must have started working—in construction. At WIK."

"Yes, of course. I'd just lost track of him by then. I had enough to think about as it was. The wedding… And then Dieter started his course. German Studies. He didn't find it particularly easy to begin with. I started working half-days, to help him while he found his feet. Then the kindergarten moved into new premises—the old building was demolished to make way for new builds, and so was the playground next to Edgar's plot. We should have just gone to the police, told them there was someone living illegally in a summer house. I don't know if that would've helped him. At least if we had then it wouldn't have happened."

"Can I ask you something? Did you like Edgar?"

"What do you mean like him? Edgar wasn't even eighteen, I was over twenty. I had Dieter. That's all there was to it. What do you think?"

That's right, Charlie, don't tell everything. There's no point in telling everything. I never did, my whole life. I didn't even tell you everything, Charlie. It's impossible to tell everything, anyway. Maybe you're not really even human if you tell everything.

"You don't have to give me an answer."

"I did like him, of course I did. He could be very funny. Touching. He was always on the go… I…"

Don't cry, Charlie. Do me a favour and don't cry. I was just a loser. I was just a regular idiot, a nutcase, a show-off and all that. Nothing to cry about. Seriously.

"I've been told to ask for Comrade Berliner."

"That's me."

"My name is Wibeau."

"Are you related to Edgar? Edgar Wibeau, who used to work with us?"

"Yes. I'm his father."

Addi! You old keen bean! How's it going? Right from the start you were my best enemy. I wound you up whenever I got the chance, and you laid into me whenever humanly possible. But now it's all in the past, I can come out and say it: You were a trouper! Our immortal souls were kindred. It's just that your brain ran on straighter rails than mine.

"It was a tragedy, what happened to Edgar. We were really quite devastated at first. A lot of things have

> become clearer to us now. Edgar was an admirable young man."

Addi, you disappoint me—and I thought you were a trouper. I didn't think you'd go along with all that bullshit people talk when someone's gone over the Jordan. Me, an admirable young man?! Schiller and Goethe and those guys—they were what you might call admirable men. Or Zaremba. Anyway it always used to do my head in when people came out with that crap about someone who'd died—what an admirable man he'd been and all that. I'd like to know who started it.

> "I'm afraid we had the wrong approach to Edgar from the start—no doubt about it. We underestimated him, myself especially as brigade leader. Right from the start all I saw in him was a show-off, a bungler, who simply wanted to make money at our expense."

Obviously I wanted to make money! When a guy can't afford to buy tapes, he needs money. And what does he do then? He goes into construction. Like they say: if you can't be arsed and your grades are shite, go and work on the railway or a building site. The railway was too much of a risk. They would've definitely asked for ID and a residence permit and all that crap. So construction it was. They'll take anyone. I knew that. It just pissed me off that the moment I walked into where Addi and Zaremba and the brigade were working—they used to renovate old flats in Berlin, a block at a time—the first thing Addi said was: I believe "Good morning" is the phrase you're looking for!

I knew his type. Ask a guy like that about Salinger or someone. I guarantee you he won't know. He'll think it's some textbook he hasn't read yet.

It might've all turned out differently if Addi had been off work that day or something. But as it was I was obviously anti the whole thing from the start. Maybe my nerves also weren't the best right then, because of the Charlie thing. It was getting to me more than I'd thought.

Addi's next move was to hand me one of those paint-roller things and ask me if I'd ever used one before. Every bloody Pioneer in the world has used one before. Which is why I point-blank refused to answer. Then he handed me a paintbrush and sent me over to Zaremba, to undercoat some windows. Obviously they were all gawping at me to see what I was going to do. But as soon as I laid eyes on Zaremba I felt better. Love at first sight, you might say. I could see straight away that the old guy was a beast.

Zaremba was over seventy. He could've retired ages ago, but here he was, still plugging away. And not just as a stand-in or anything. He could clamp a stepladder between his legs and genuinely dance around the room on it without even breaking a sweat. Though he basically only consisted of skin, bone and muscles anyway, so where would the sweat have come from? One trick he had was to get someone to drop an open penknife onto his biceps. It bounced off like it had hit rubber. He also used to do an impression of the Hunchback of Notre-Dame. He'd take out one of his eyes (he had a glass eye), bend at the hip and stagger around all over the place. He had us in stitches constantly. He'd picked up the glass eye fighting in Spain; someone in Philadelphia had made it for him. And he was also missing a chunk off his little finger, and two ribs—though he did still have all his teeth and both arms and a chestful of tattoos. His tattoos weren't of fat women and hearts and anchors and stuff like that. They were all flags and stars and hammer-and-sickles, and even a bit of the Kremlin Wall. I think he must've been from Bohemia or something originally. But the greatest thing was that he still got with women. I don't know if you believe me, guys, but it was a true fact. Zaremba was in charge of our trailer. He was the one that cleaned it, so he always had the key. It was a pretty snazzy vehicle.

Two bunks, the whole shebang. One evening after dark I snuck up to it—I didn't know anything at that point, it was just that I had a particular reason for needing to go under the trailer that night—and I clearly heard him getting it on with this woman. I reckon she must've been really nice, judging by her laugh. But don't think I was automatically going to start worshipping Zaremba on bended knee because of all that. No way. Partly because the first thing he asked me was whether I was paid up with the union. He was the treasurer. That always used to do my head in. If it'd been anyone else I would've turned my back on them straight away. But as it was I just held out my membership book. He took it off me and started nosing through it. He probably just wanted to know what the deal was with me. Obviously I hadn't paid since I'd got to Berlin. He immediately hoicked out this funny metal box, the idea being for me to pay up to date. Which would've been quite a feat considering I couldn't even afford to buy tapes. He probably just wanted to know that.

So then I got on with undercoating one of these windows. The paint kept running onto the glass. I'd painted the windows millions of times at home but this time I just couldn't seem to get it right. If they hadn't all been gawping at me so much to see how I was doing, I would've been able to bash out a really decent window. Not as decent as Zaremba. Zaremba painted like a machine. But as decent as any of the rest of them, including Addi. Addi was getting flustered, you could tell. The only reason he didn't go apeshit right there and then was because Zaremba was standing next to me. I quickly realized that Zaremba wasn't going to lose his cool. He wasn't even looking at me. Anyway, Addi eventually got to the point where he couldn't take it any more and burst out: Why not paint over the whole window while you're at it?!

You can probably guess what I did then. I started painting over the whole window. I thought Addi was going to fall off his ladder. But then *I* nearly fell off my ladder—or I would've if I'd been on one. Zaremba, who was stood right next to me, suddenly started singing! I felt like I'd been kicked by a horse and hit by a bus and everything at the same time. Zaremba's voice came blasting out, and a second later the rest of them joined in. It wasn't a pop song or anything—it was one of those songs you only ever know the first verse of. But this crew managed to blast out the entire thing. It went something like: "Arise, Socialists! Close the ranks! The flags are flying, the drumbeat calls…"

What a crew, guys! Arise, Socialists! I nearly dropped the bloody paintbrush. This was basically Zaremba's tactic for when dear old Addi was about to go apeshit. That became clear the next time it happened, which was in some old kitchen somewhere. The wall was quite cracked, and I was s'posed to plaster it up. Addi said: Ever worked with plaster before? Then come and have a look at this wall.

In that vein.

So I started mixing up some plaster in this bucket. I don't know if you've ever done it, guys? Anyway every time I ever did it I always started off by putting in too much water, then too much plaster, and so on. So the bucket kept getting fuller and fuller and I would've had to have been some kind of plastering genius to stop the stuff going hard. I was starting to look like a bit of a moron, until I was saved by Addi. He lost it. He hissed at me: Why not fill the whole *bucket* while you're at it?

That was the best he could come up with. Naturally I took him at his word and tipped all of the plaster into the bucket. At almost the exact same moment, Zaremba started singing. He couldn't even see us from the bog or wherever it was he was hiding. But he must've been able to smell what was going on. It was another one of those mental songs, this time with partisans, and again he got the whole crew joining in. He had them well trained. Addi pulled himself together almost immediately and sent me into one of the bedrooms to sweep the floor ready for undercoating. If I was him I probably would've tipped the whole bloody bucket of plaster over my head. But Addi pulled himself together. That was my light-bulb moment—I suddenly twigged what the whole singing thing was all about. I vacated the area. I was just curious to know what Zaremba would do if I behaved like that to him. Whether he'd still sing then. But first I heard Zaremba go charging into the kitchen and growl at Addi: Got to calm down, lad. Really calm down. Ey?

And Addi: Tell me, what exactly does he want from us? He wants to make money at our expense, that's what. No doubt about it. He's a waste of space.

And Zaremba went: Ey... Waste of space?!

I think I already mentioned that Zaremba came from Bohemia. Which probably explains that "Ey" thing. He used it at least three times in every sentence. The guy could say more with that "Ey" than other people do in whole novels. When he said "Ey?" with his head on one side, it meant: Think it over, Comrade! When he went "Ey?!" while raising his caterpillar eyebrows, it meant: Don't say that again, pal! When he said it with his little pig-eyes squinched shut, everyone knew he was about to do his Hunchback of Notre-Dame impression. I don't know if it's true or not but someone told me that right after 'forty-five Zaremba was chief judge in Berlin for three weeks. Apparently he passed some really weird and really tough sentences. Ey? Mr Defendant, you were always a great friend to Communism, sawaiyeer? That kind of thing. "Sawaiyeer" was another one of his words. It took me ages to figure out that "sawaiyeer" meant "so I hear". Zaremba was a total beast.

I don't know whether he'd had enough of singing or whether he realized that me and Addi weren't getting on, but anyway he started giving me jobs himself. The first one was to limewash the ceiling and the panelling, or rather the bit above the panelling, in some bloody bog. He left me to do it on my own, and I mixed up this beautiful blue gloop and started decorating the walls and ceiling with the roller, Pop Art style. By the end it looked like a set of designs for motorway interchanges. And all in this beautiful shade of blue. I was just getting really into the swing of it when I realized Zaremba was standing there, with the rest of the crew behind him. They were probably super-curious to know what he was going to do with me, especially Addi. But all he said was "Ey?!"

That must've been the longest "Ey" I ever heard him say. And on top of that he put his head on one side, raised his caterpillar eyebrows and squinched up his little pig-eyes. I could've pissed myself laughing. I'm still proud of that new "Ey"-variant, to this day.

> "He certainly did behave strangely. No doubt about it. But that in itself should have given us food for thought—myself especially. Instead I drove him out; even Zaremba couldn't prevent it. Zaremba may have been the only one of us with any idea what Edgar was capable of. But I was too blinkered. It was to do with our MSPM—Mistless Spray Paint Machine. We'd already built several other things, but this was going to be our greatest yet. A machine that could spray any type of paint, without giving off any of that harmful mist you still get with those kinds of machines. It would have been unique, even on the international market. But unfortunately we'd come to a standstill with it just then. Not even the experts we ended up calling in could get any further with it. And while all this was going on, along came Edgar and started sticking his oar in. I'm afraid I lost my temper. I'm not trying to excuse myself. I just wasn't quite all there."

Do me a favour, Addi, and give it a rest. I can tell you exactly what I was "capable of": nothing. And nothing at *all* when it came to the MSPM. Your idea with the compressed air and the hollow nozzle was no good, and my hydraulics idea was no good either. So why all the wailing and gnashing of teeth? I'll admit I really did think hydraulics was the way to go, right from the start in fact—pretty much the moment I set eyes on the thing. It was lying around under our trailer. I'd tripped over it at least three times, and I'd already given it the once-over, but I would rather've chewed my own arm off than ask anyone what kind of machine it was and stuff. Especially Addi. Till one day Zaremba just came out with it of his own accord. That bastard could see through me like glass, I reckon.

Never seen one before, ey? No way you could've done, either. It's unique. This spray machine sprays every type of paint under the sun, does as much in three hours as three painters can do in a day, ey, and it does all that without giving off any mist, making it superior to any machine of its kind on the market, even American ones, sawaiyeer.—Once we get it working, that is, ey?

Then he flicked a bit of dust off the thing and stood around sighing for a bit. And then he said: It's not our first invention, but it is our best, ey.

I got the impression he was trying to give Addi and Co.—who obviously had all come clustering round—a bit of a kick up the arse. The thing had probably just been lying around for a while now. It didn't work at all: it spewed out clouds and clouds of mist, and that was it.

I said: The Machine shall never replace it. At the same time I held my paintbrush up in the air. And then I started undercoating again.

Immediately, Addi went off on one: Listen up, my friend. That's all well and good. I don't know what it is you've got such a bee in your bonnet about, but there's obviously something. No doubt about that. I don't care what it is. But we're a team, and a good one too, and you're part of it now. And in the long run you'll find you don't have much choice but to toe the line and pull your weight. And don't think you'd be our first convert. There've been plenty of others before you that we've knocked into shape. Just ask Jonas. Anyway, we've yet to see the man who can drag us down to the average.

There ended the lesson. He turned on his heel and went charging off with the rest of them in tow. I only understood about half of it. My little joke about the machine had been pretty harmless, after all. I had lots of other stuff up my sleeve. Old Werther, for example. I quickly analysed the situation and realized I'd hit on Addi's weakest point with the spray machine.

Then Zaremba chipped in: You've got to understand him, ey. The spray machine was his idea. For Christ's sake don't mess with it. It's either going to be a great success or a terrible failure, ey? His first!

Me:

He is the most punctilious fool one could ever meet—advancing one step at a time, fussing like an old woman—a man who is never satisfied with himself and whom it is thus impossible for anybody else to please.

Old Werther was back at last. Zaremba opened his little pig-eyes wide and growled: Ey! Don't you go saying that!

He was the first person not to be completely thrown by that Old High German stuff. I would've felt bad if he had been. I'll admit I did pick out a relatively normal bit for him. I don't know if you get me, guys. Then a couple of days later it all came to a head. Addi and the gang set up the spray machine in the yard behind one of these old blocks of flats, and hooked it all up. Two experts had come along from this speciality shop with a whole box full of nozzles, all different types, which were going to be tested out. It was a big occasion. All kinds of people showed up. All the potters and brickies and everyone else that was knocking around in those buildings. Not one of the nozzles worked. Either a jet as thick as your arm came shooting out, or the thing misted like a lawn sprinkler. The experts weren't super-optimistic, even to begin with, but they dutifully handed over every one of their nozzles. Addi just would not let it go. He was a tenacious bastard. Till the moment he tried out the smallest-calibre nozzle, and the pressure was just too much for it. The bloody hose burst and suddenly everyone within a ten-metre radius was as yellow as a Chinaman or something. Especially Addi. There was general hilarity.

The experts said: Best leave it. It didn't go any better when we tried it, and we've got everything! It can't be done! Technologically impossible—for the time being at least. The nozzles are not the issue.

Then I drew my Werther pistol:

The human race is a monotonous affair. Most people spend the greater part of their time working in order to live, and what little freedom they have left inspires in them such great alarm that they will use any means within their power to be rid of it.

The experts probably thought I was the brigade clown. They grinned, anyway. But the brigade itself came slowly towards me, with Addi leading the way. They were still wiping the yellow gloop off their faces. I put my dukes up just in case, but nothing happened. Addi just hissed coldly: Get out of here. Just get out of here, or I won't be responsible for my actions.

I couldn't see his face properly. I still had paint in my eyes. But it really did sound like he was about to cry. Addi was over twenty years old. I couldn't remember when the last time I'd cried was. It'd been quite a while ago anyway. Perhaps that's why I did in fact get out of there pretty speedily. Maybe I'd gone too far or something. I hope you don't think I was being a wimp, guys. In boxing you're not really allowed to defend yourself anyway. If you throw a stupid punch they stop the fight straight away. Plus Zaremba was there, and he signalled to me that I should make myself scarce, that it was the best thing to do just then. So that, for the time being, was the end of my guest stint as a painter with Addi and Co.

It happened to be pissing it down that day. I legged it back to my kolkhoz. The first thing I did when I got back was to dictate the following onto the new tape for Old Willi:

And it is the fault of all of you, who talked me into taking up the yoke and who extolled at such great length the virtues of activity. Activity!... I have tendered my resignation... I pray you break the news gently to my mother. End.

I felt like that fitted the situation perfectly.

"I fired him, just like that! It's not that we were exclusive or anything—Jonas, for example, had just got out of prison when he joined us. But we do get a lot of people coming to us who can't, and usually don't want to, do very much. It's not easy to build up a brigade that you can really start to achieve something with."

"There's no need to apologize! Perhaps Edgar was just a bit of a nutcase, an oddball—perhaps he was grumpy all the time, and incapable of fitting in, and lazy, I don't know…"

"Steady on! He was never grumpy, actually—not with us anyway. And an oddball?… But you know him better than I do."

"Know him? I haven't seen him since he was five years old!"

"Ah, I didn't know that. Although—wait a minute! Edgar went to visit you. He went to your flat!"

Shut up, Addi!

"He came back raving about it. Your studio flat, north-facing, pictures everywhere, gloriously bohemian…"

I said shut *up*, Addi!

"...Pardon me. I didn't hear this from Edgar—Zaremba told me about it."

"When's this supposed to have been?"

"It must have been after we'd fired him. End of October."

"He never came to my flat."

I did though, I'm afraid. I don't even know why I went there, but I did. He lived in one of those gorgeous tiled tower blocks that have started springing up all over Berlin. I knew his address. But I didn't know it was one of those gorgeous tower blocks. He had a flat there. And it's true it was north-facing. I'm sure you guys don't think I was stupid enough to march straight up and introduce myself. Hi, Dad, I'm Edgar, that kind of thing. No way. I had my work clothes on. When he opened the door I just told him I was the heating engineer. He wasn't massively thrilled about it but he believed me, no questions asked. I don't know what I would've done if he hadn't believed me. I didn't have any kind of plan, but still I was pretty sure it was all going to work out OK. Whack on a pair of blue trousers and you're the heating engineer. A bloody jacket, and you're the new caretaker. A leather bag and you're the guy from the telephone exchange. And so on. They'll believe anything, and you can't even blame them. You just need to know how to pull it off. Also I still had a hammer with me. I clanged away at the bathroom radiator with it for a bit, while he stood in the doorway and watched me. I didn't say anything. I just needed some time to get used to him. Do you know what I mean, guys? Knowing you've got a father and actually seeing him are not *at all* the same thing. He looked about thirty or so. That came as a massive shock to me. I had no idea. I'd always thought he was at least fifty! I don't even know why. He stood there in the doorway in his dressing gown and a pair of brand-new jeans. I noticed that straight away. Around that time, real jeans had suddenly appeared in Berlin. No idea why, but they had. Something was about to go down. Obviously word got round straight away—in certain circles at least. They were selling them in the rear annexe of some house, because they knew there was no department store in Berlin big enough to hold the crowds that would turn out for those jeans. And they were right. As I'm sure you've guessed, guys, there was no way I was going to miss that. I was there with bells on. It was ages since I'd got up as early as I did that day, to make sure I got there in time. I would've been kicking myself like a bastard if I hadn't got any jeans. There were about three thousand of us standing there in the hallway waiting to be let in. You can't even imagine how squished we were. That day the first snow of the year fell, but I can tell you for a fact not one of us felt cold. A couple of people had brought some music along. The atmosphere was like at Christmas, just before you're allowed to look under the tree and start opening your presents—if you still believe in Father Christmas, that is. We were all on a massive high. I was just about to launch into my "Bluejeans" song when they opened the door, and it was showtime. Behind the door were four fully grown salesmen. We shoved them the hell out of the way and lobbed ourselves at the jeans. Sadly, we were disappointed. The ones they had weren't the real sort. They were authentic jeans, but they weren't the real sort. Still, the whole event turned out pretty well. I reckon the best bit was these two mums from somewhere out in the sticks who were standing with us in the hallway. They wanted to get some real jeans to take back to their little sonnykins in the arse end of nowhere. But the atmosphere gradually got more and more crazy, and suddenly they started shitting themselves. The poor dears wanted out of there. There wasn't a snowball's chance in hell of that happening—even if I or anyone else had wanted to help them. They had to go along with it, like it or not. I hope they came out of it more or less in one piece.

Anyway, this father of mine must have been somewhere in the crowd that day. I could picture it easily, what with him standing right there in front of me keeping an eye on me from the doorway. And the reason he was standing there was clear to me pretty much straight away. In the bathroom, hanging on a clothesline, was a pair of stockings. He blatantly had a woman in his bedroom, and *that* was the room I wanted to look round before telling him who I was. So I said: All fine in here. Let's see how the bedroom's looking.

Him: It's all fine in there too.

Me: I'm sure it is—but this is the last time we'll be visiting this year.

Then he gave in, and we went through into the bedroom. The woman was in bed. Next to the bed was this camp bed which was where he must've slept. I liked the woman straight away. Something about her reminded me of Charlie. I couldn't think what. Probably the way she looked directly at you the whole time, the way she kept her dazzlers constantly fixed on you. Straight away I could picture how it would've been with the three of us living together. We would've got a bigger bed, and I would've slept in the hallway on the old one—or on the camp bed, I wouldn't have minded. I would've gone out to get rolls in the morning and made coffee and we would've had breakfast all together on their bed. And in the evenings I would've dragged them both along to the *Große Melodie*, or even just her on her own, and we would've flirted a bit. Not in a bad way, though, obviously—just as friends.

I immediately turned on the charm: Beg your pardon, madam. Just the heating engineer. Won't be a minute. That kind of thing.

Then I got cracking on the radiator. I tapped out a bit of Morse code on the pipes with my hammer and listened to the echo, the way those heating blokes do. At the same time, obviously, I was scoping out the entire room. There wasn't a lot in it. Portable shelves with books on. A TV, the one before the latest model. Not one single picture on the walls. The woman offered me a cigarette.

I said: No thanks. Smoking is a major obstacle to communication.

I was going for a sort of "professional young tradesman" vibe. Then I asked this father: You're not a big fan of pictures, then?

He was lost.

I went on: I mean—the walls. Tabula rasa. Us guys see a lot of flats. They've got pictures all over the place, all kinds of stuff, whereas you...But then you do have other nice things instead.

The woman smiled. She'd understood straight away. It probably wasn't difficult, to be fair. We looked at each other for a second. I remember thinking she was the only thing in the room that wasn't doing my head in. Everything else was. Especially the bare walls. That's the only reason I can think of why I would've suddenly started blathering like a moron: But that's the way it should be. I always say if you're going to have pictures they should be ones you've painted yourself—and obviously it looks a bit cocky to put your own pictures up all over the place. Do you have children, if you don't mind me asking? One tip about children: they're awesome at painting. You can put as much of their stuff on the wall as you like without feeling embarrassed...

I don't even know what other ridiculous crap I came out with. I don't think I stopped talking till I was standing outside on the stairs again and the door was shut and I realized I hadn't said a word about who I was and stuff. But I just couldn't bring myself to ring the bell again and tell them everything. I don't know if you get me, guys.

After that I crawled back into my shack, as usual. I wanted to put some music on and stuff and I did, it's just that for some reason it wasn't zinging. I knew myself well enough by then to figure out that there was something wrong with me. I did some quick self-analysis and realized that what I wanted to do was start building my *own* spray machine, right there and then. My *own* MSPM. I didn't know how yet. I just knew it would have to look completely different from Addi's. I knew it wouldn't be easy without proper tools and stuff. But I was never one to be put off by those kinds of difficulties. It was also clear to me that the whole thing would have to be done in secret. And then once my spray machine was working I'd go and drop in on the brigade, super-nonchalant and everything like some lord. I don't know if you get me, guys. Anyway that exact same day, like the idiot that I was, I started combing the whole bloody godforsaken allotment for bits I might be able to use. I don't know if you can imagine all the stuff you find kicking around on an allotment. All sorts, guys, I can tell you—just not the stuff I needed. But I still schlepped everything back with me that looked like it might be of some use. The first thing to do is get hold of your materials, I thought. That was the first stone on my grave, guys. The first nail in my coffin.

"I could say we brought him back into the fold fairly quickly. But it was mainly on Zaremba's initiative. And it was already too late, really. By that time Edgar had already started working on his own MSPM.

Even Zaremba didn't know the whole story. We went and tracked him down in his summer house. But we didn't see any sign that he was building a spray machine. And I'm afraid we just didn't think to look in the kitchen."

Thinking to look in the kitchen wouldn't have got you anywhere—it was locked. I wouldn't have let anyone in. Maybe not even Charlie. I was merrily building away when I saw Zaremba's skull with his mouldy hair pop up from behind my hedge. I battened down the hatches straight away, guys. I chucked myself down on the bloody sofa and started coughing. It wasn't that I was ill or anything, not properly anyway. I did have a cough. I'd probably picked it up during my rummagings on the bloody allotment. And I should maybe have started heating the place by then. But I could've stopped coughing if I'd wanted to. The thing was, I'd got really into the habit of it. I liked the effect it created. Edgar Wibeau, the unrecognized genius, working away selflessly on his latest invention, half his lung eaten away and still he doesn't give up. I was a complete and utter idiot, seriously. But it spurred me on. I don't know if you get me, guys. So anyway there I was coughing like a pro as the brigade came storming into my shack. Actually, they didn't storm in. They came in pretty quietly. First Addi, then Zaremba. The old guy was probably pushing him from behind. The two of them obviously thought they should feel guilty about me or something. Because they'd kicked me out. And then there I was on the sofa with my cough! I don't know if you guys can imagine how much of an expert I was at that cough. And I also had my feet poking out from under the bloody blanket as if it was too short.

Zaremba went: Ahoy! Can't you cough any louder? Then he turned away to let Addi say his piece. First of all Addi looked for something to hang onto, then off he went: What I wanted to say was—I might come across as a bit blunt sometimes, that's just my way, no doubt about it. We'll both have to bear it in mind in future. And the spray machine is in the past now. That ship has sailed, no doubt about it.

It wasn't easy for him. I was almost moved. I couldn't say anything though because of the cough. Jonas, the reformed character, took care of the rest: We thought you could specialize in floors. You can do them with a roller no problem. And Saturday evenings we all go bowling.

In the meantime, of course, the rest of the gang had all come clustering round as well. They'd trickled in one by one. I got the feeling Zaremba or Addi had had them standing guard on all four sides of the shack in case I tried to go AWOL. I could've pissed myself laughing. They stood there gawping at my collected works. I could see they were pretty blown away. From that moment on they treated me like a rare bird or something, that you shouldn't get too close to. Apart from Zaremba. Old Zaremba definitely had his suspicions. He started sniffing around my shack as well at that point. Eventually he tried the kitchen door handle. But like I said, it was locked, and all the questions he asked to try and catch me out—like whether I was going to spend the winter here, for example—I couldn't really answer. This cough of mine was just so unpredictable. It always flared up at the most awkward moments, guys. I really was an expert at it. Zaremba wanted to send me to the doctor's straight away, the bastard. For a moment I sat there like a bit of a lemon. Then it occurred to me that I used to get this cough every autumn, and it was totally harmless. An allergy. Hay fever of the throat or something. The only known case of its kind. A mystery of science. And then Zaremba eventually let it go. But my cough improved dramatically after that—what I mean is, it went away, apart from occasional minor attacks. I needed a doctor like I needed a flipping hole in the head, guys. My opinion on doctors was that they could piss right off. I only once went to see a doctor voluntarily, about a rash on my feet. Half an hour later I was lying on his table and he was stabbing two syringes into each of my toes and pulling my toenails off. That in itself was outrageous. But then once he'd finished with me, if you can believe this, guys, he shoved me out into the waiting room on foot. I was bleeding through the bandages like a madman. He didn't even think to give me a wheelchair or anything. Since then I've had very set opinions on doctors.

Anyway, from that day onwards I was on the endangered species list where Addi was concerned. First the pictures, then the cough that was the only one of its kind in the world. I could probably've got away with even more after that. But I managed to control myself. I wasn't exactly mad keen for them to pay another visit to my kolkhoz, and possibly find out about my spray machine. I was that much of an idiot, I always thought I was going to make it big with the spray machine. I denied myself practically everything. I didn't even draw my Werther pistol once, for example. I dutifully painted my floors with the roller, and even went bowling with them on Saturdays. I sat there like a cat on hot bricks or something, while they bowled and thought to themselves: We've done a great job of bringing young Wibeau into line. It was almost like being back in Mittenberg. And at home my spray machine was waiting.

Around that time I also figured out where the Huguenot museum was, just by chance. I'd actually given up looking for it long before. At the beginning I'd asked loads of people, a sort of public poll. Could you tell me where I might find the Huguenot museum? Success rate zero. No bastard in Berlin knew anything about it. Most of them probably thought I was either a dumb-arse or a tourist. And then all of a sudden I found myself standing right in front of it. It was in a ruined church. The church had caught my attention because it was the first bombed building I'd ever seen. In Mittenberg no one had so much as fired a shot! General Brusilov or whatever his name was had practically forgotten to occupy the place. Anyway the one doorway in the whole building that was still intact had a sign saying "Huguenot Museum". And below that: "Closed for renovation". Normally I wouldn't have taken any notice of that sign. I was a Huguenot, after all, and they couldn't shut me out. In fact I was pretty sure the curator would've welcomed me with open arms. A real live Huguenot descendant! As far as I knew we were a dying breed. But for some reason I turned back when I saw that sign. I did some quick self-analysis and realized that it just didn't interest me any more whether I was of noble blood or not, or what the other Huguenots were up to; probably not even whether I was a Huguenot or a Mormon or anything else. For some reason it just didn't interest me any more.

But I did come up with another equally stupid idea around the same time. I decided to write to Charlie.

Since that last day I'd hardly seen her at all. It was clear to me she'd made it up with Dieter long ago and that I had no chance with her after all. But she was still on my mind the entire time. I don't know if you get me, guys. My first thought, straight away, was Old Werther. He was always writing letters to that Charlotte of his. It didn't take me long to find a suitable one:

If you could see me, dearest, amidst this whirl of distractions! How dry and withered my senses become;... not a single hour of bliss! Nothing! Nothing!

I wrote it out carefully on the back of a menu in that bowling alley. But I never sent it. I'd realized Werther wasn't going to get me anywhere with Charlie any more. I couldn't just keep wheeling him out every five minutes. Only I couldn't think what else to do. I couldn't just go and see her. Then one evening there was an envelope in my letter box. I could see it from quite a long way away. Usually all my letters got sent to my PO box. There was no stamp on it either. And inside there was a card from

Charlie: Are you still alive? Come and see us sometime. We got married a while back.

So Charlie must've been there in person. That nearly killed me, guys. My knees went all wobbly. Seriously. I got the shivers. I dropped everything and went charging off straight away. Eight minutes later I was at Dieter's door. I just assumed they'd both be living at his now. And I was right. Charlie opened the door. At first she just stared at me. I got the feeling I wasn't entirely welcome right then. I mean, I was welcome, but not *entirely* welcome. Maybe she just hadn't thought I'd show up the exact same day she'd brought the letter to my kolkhoz. But anyway, she invited me into the room. They only had one room. In the room was Dieter. He was sitting there behind his desk in exactly the same position as a few weeks before. Or rather, he was sitting in front of it. He had the desk pushed up against the window and he was sitting in front of it with his back to the room. I understood that completely. When you've only got one room, and you have to work in it as well, you need to be able to block yourself off somehow. And Dieter did that with his back. His back was basically a wall.

Charlie said: Turn round!

Dieter turned round, and luckily it occurred to me to say: Just wanted to see if you've got a pipe wrench I could borrow.

I just couldn't help feeling that Dieter wasn't actually supposed to know Charlie had invited me over. I didn't take more than one step inside the room. Weirdly, Charlie said: Do we have a pipe wrench?

I swiftly analysed the situation and came to the conclusion that Charlie was playing along with the pipe wrench thing. I immediately got the shivers again. Dieter asked: What d'you need a pipe wrench for? Burst pipe?

Me: You could say that.

It just so happened that I did actually need a wrench. For the spray machine. I'd managed to track down the kind of thing I wanted in some old shed, only it was so wrecked that the most you would've been able to do with it was bash a hole in your own knee. Then we shook mitts, and Dieter went: Well?

That was his Uncle Dieter-style "well". He might as well have added: "… young man. Have we mended our ways since our last meeting, or is our head still full of these foolish notions?" Usually stuff like that would've made me go off the deep end, guys, and this was no exception. But I composed myself and brought myself back down to earth and went back to being the humble, sensible, mature young man I'd recently become, guys. I don't know if you can imagine it—me being humble. And all because, like the idiot that I was, I thought I had the spray machine up my sleeve. I can't even remember what I was actually thinking. I must've just been so sure about my hydraulics idea that before I'd even tested it out I was already as humble as a great inventor after a big success. The great Edgar Wibeau, such a likeable young man, still so modest even after everything he's achieved, et cetera, et cetera. Like with these top athletes. Man, I was an idiot, guys. And also, obviously, I could see Charlie turning red. I mean, I couldn't *see* it. I couldn't even look at her the whole time, or else I probably would've done something massively stupid. But I was *aware* of it. She probably thought her greatest dream was coming true—that me and Dieter were becoming good friends. Up to that point she'd been standing behind me in the doorway. Now she got all excited and wanted to make tea and stuff and told me to sit myself down. The room was unrecognizable. It hadn't just been redecorated and stuff—it'd been completely refurbished. I don't mean with furniture. Actually all that was new were the pictures and lamps and curtains and all kinds of little bits and bobs that Charlie had probably brought with her when she moved in. Suddenly it was somewhere I would've wanted to live. I'm not saying it was all colour-coordinated. The armchairs matching the rug, the rug matching the curtains, the curtains matching the wallpaper and the wallpaper matching the armchairs. Stuff like that always used to do my head in. It wasn't that. But the pictures, for example, had all been done by the kids from the kindergarten. I probably already mentioned that kids are shit-hot at painting. One of the pictures looked like it was s'posed to be a snowman. He was drawn all in red. He looked like a sort of Charlie Chaplin who'd had all his clothes nicked. He could really get to you. Hung up next to the snowman was Dieter's air rifle. All the books suddenly looked like they were constantly being read by someone. You suddenly wanted to go and plop yourself down somewhere and read them all one after the other. I started whizzing around the room looking at everything and talking about it. I praised everything like a madman. My only advice to anyone who fancies a girl, or a woman, is that you've got to praise her. That was all just part of the service with me. Not in an awkward way, obviously—more like the way I was doing in that room of Charlie's, for example. Apart from the fact that I genuinely did like it, I'd obviously also noticed that Charlie was going red and white by turns. I thought it was quite possible Dieter still hadn't said a word about any of it. And as if to confirm the fact, he soon started to block himself off again. He'd gone back to work. When Charlie saw that she sat down straight away, and I had to as well. It nearly killed me. She still did that thing with her skirt when she sat down. I can't even describe what I was feeling, guys. A bit later she ushered me out of the room. Outside, she explained: You've got to understand him, you know? He's *completely* out of the loop with everything, what with being in the army so long. He's the oldest in his year group. I think he's still not sure whether Literature's the right course for him. She was practically whispering. Then she asked me: And what about you? How's the summer house?

I automatically started having one of my coughing fits—discreetly, of course.

Charlie, straight off: You're not planning to spend the winter there, surely?

Me: It's unlikely.

I really was an expert at that cough.

Then she asked me: Are you working?

Me: Of course. In construction.

I could clearly see that floated her boat. Charlie was one of those people you can ask whether they believe in "the good in people", and they'll say yes without a blush. And just then she was probably thinking that the good in me had triumphed and that maybe it was because she'd drummed her opinion into me so soundly that time.

Whenever I read in some book that someone suddenly found themselves somewhere and they were s'posed to be so distracted that they didn't know how they got there, it usually made me zone out straight away. I used to think it was complete bullshit. But that evening I found myself standing outside my shack and I genuinely didn't know how I'd got there. I must've been asleep the whole way or something. I whacked the tape player on as soon as I got in. At first I wanted to spend half the night dancing, but then I started tinkering away like a madman at my spray machine. That night I was more certain than ever that I was on the right track with the spray machine. I was just sorry I hadn't actually brought the pipe wrench back with me from Charlie's—the subject hadn't come up again, obviously. The one I had really was a piece of shit. But it did at least give me an excuse to show up at Charlie's again the next day. Dieter was out. Charlie was fiddling about with one of her ceiling lampshades. She couldn't get it to stay on. She was standing on a stepladder like the ones we had on site. One of the ones Old Zaremba could dance on. I hoicked myself up onto the other side of the ladder, and we both worked away at this stupid lampshade. Charlie held and I screwed. But believe it or not, guys, my hand was shaking. I just couldn't get that grub screw to hold. After all, I had

Charlie closer to me than ever before. Even then I still might've managed it. Except that she also had her dazzlers fixed right on me. It got to the point where I held and Charlie screwed. That was the best thing for the screw, at any rate. It finally held. Me and Charlie both felt like our arms were about to drop off. Have you guys ever had that when you've been holding your arms up in the air for hours? Anyone who paints ceilings or puts up curtains will know what I'm talking about. We groaned in unison and massaged our arms, all while standing on the ladder. Then I started telling her about Zaremba and how he could dance on the ladder, and we grabbed onto each other's arms and started wobbling around the room on the ladder. We nearly toppled over at least three times, but we'd decided to try and make it all the way to the door without getting off, and we did. I talked her into it. That was the thing—you could talk Charlie into something like that. Ninety-nine out of a hundred women would've bailed out straight away, or shrieked about for a bit and then jumped off. Not Charlie. When we got to the door we found Dieter standing there. We leapt off the ladder straight away. Charlie asked him: Do you want something to eat?

Me: I'll get going then. I just popped round to get the pipe wrench.

I was super-afraid he was going to grab hold of Charlie right in front of my eyes and maybe kiss her or something. I don't know what would've happened then, guys. But nothing could've been further from Dieter's mind. He went over to his desk, briefcase in hand. Either he never kissed Charlie when he got in or he was holding back this time because of me. It immediately made me think of something Old Werther wrote to his mate Wilhelm:

And he is so honest a man as to have never once kissed Lotte in my presence. May God reward him for it.

I didn't understand what being honest had to do with it, but I understood all the rest. I would never in my life have thought I'd come to understand this Werther so well. Anyway, Dieter would've had a hard time kissing Charlie or anything else. She pretty much legged it into the kitchen. I should still have left, obviously. But I stayed. I put the ladder away. Then I loitered about in the room. I wanted to start up a conversation with Dieter, but I just couldn't think of anything. Suddenly I was holding the air rifle. Dieter didn't say a word. And when Charlie came back with a snack for him she said straight away: Here's an idea, guys. After this we can all go and do a bit of shooting, up at the railway embankment. You always said you were going to teach me.

Dieter grunted: Not enough light for shooting at this hour.

He was against it. He wanted to work. He thought it was kids' stuff. Just like our ladder-dancing. But Charlie fixed her dazzlers on him, and he gave in.

What sucked for him was that he just didn't join in properly when we got to the embankment. I managed to quickly track down an old No Parking sign, and we shot at that. Or rather, Charlie shot. Dieter announced the hits and misses, and I corrected Charlie's technique. We ended up doing it that way round because Dieter didn't even think to pay any attention to Charlie. He left the children to their games, so to speak. He was probably thinking about all the time this was costing him.

I could understand him, in a way, but I still went to town on helping Charlie. I showed her how to steady the butt against her shoulder, how to stand with her feet at right angles and how to start off high and come down towards the target while breathing out, and all that stuff they teach you in military training. Full sight, fine sight, proper bead and trigger slack and all that. Charlie shot and shot and was quite happy to let me pull her about, until she noticed what was up with Dieter—or until she *wanted* to notice, maybe. Then she stopped. Anyway, Dieter did actually have a point—it had been too dark for quite a while. But he had to promise to go on an outing with her the next Sunday, it didn't matter where, just as long as they got out of the house. There was no mention of me going, at least not outright. Charlie was very clever about it. She said: Let's go on an outing.

It could've meant anything. But maybe like an idiot I just imagined it did. Maybe she didn't mean me at all. Maybe everything that happened after that wouldn't have happened if I hadn't imagined, like an idiot, that Charlie had invited me as well. But I don't regret it, any of it. I don't regret it at all.

The next Sunday I was sat next to Charlie on the sofa in their room. It was raining like mad. Dieter was sat at his desk working, and we were waiting for him to finish. Charlie already had her raincoat on and everything. She hadn't been at all surprised or anything when I'd rung the doorbell. So I'd been right after all. Or maybe she was surprised, but she didn't show it. This time Dieter was *writing*. With two fingers. On the typewriter. Whatever he was writing, he was composing it as he went along. An essay, I reckoned, and I was probably right. I could see straight away that it wasn't going well. I knew the feeling. He was typing about one letter every half-hour. That says it all, guys. In the end Charlie said: You can't *force* it!

Dieter made no comment. I couldn't help looking at his legs the whole time. He'd wrapped them round the chair legs and got himself firmly hooked on by the feet. I didn't know if that was just a habit of his. But it'd been obvious to me from the start, really, that he wasn't going to come with us.

Charlie tried again: Come on! Why not just take a break from it for now? That can work wonders!

She wasn't angry or anything. Not yet. She was about as gentle as a nurse is s'posed to be.

Dieter said: It's not really boating weather.

I don't know if I already mentioned that Charlie wanted to hire out a boat.

Charlie said straight away: Well not a boat then—a steamer.

Dieter was right, really. Taking a boat out in that weather was a nuts idea.

He started typing again.

Charlie: Not a steamer then. We'll just go round the block a few times.

It was her last offer, and this really was Dieter's chance. But he didn't move.

Charlie: Anyway, it's not like we're made of sugar.

I think that was the moment she lost patience. Dieter said calmly: You two go.

And Charlie: You promised!

Dieter: I already said, you two can go!

Then Charlie's voice rose: Fine, we will!

I left at that point. Anyone could see what was going to happen next. I was totally out of place there. What I mean is I left the room. I should have completely left, of course. I realize that. But I just couldn't bring myself to. I loitered about in the kitchen. It suddenly made me think of something Old Werther had written:

Do not his wretched business affairs occupy him more than that precious, charming woman?... Complacency is what it is, and indifference!

Now Dieter was no businessman and Charlie was anything but a "precious, charming woman". And it wasn't complacency with Dieter either. True, he got a big grant because he'd been in the army, but I bet us guys earned three times as much by slapping a bit of paint on the wall. I didn't know what it was. In theory I had no beef with Dieter. But one thing was for certain—he hadn't actually gone out anywhere with Charlie for yonks. That was the one thing that was certain. Pretty much the moment I'd finished analysing it, Charlie came shooting out of the room. I mean it when I say shooting, guys. All she said to me was: Come on!

I was beside her in a flash.

Then she said: Wait!

I waited. She took this grey cape thing down off the coat hook and thrust it at my chest. Dieter must've brought it back with him from the army. It smelt like chewing gum mixed with petrol, cheese and burnt rubbish.

She asked me: Can you drive a motorboat?

I said: Not so much.

Normally I would've said: Course I can. But I was getting so good at the civilized-young-man act that I just came straight out and told the truth.

Charlie asked: What's wrong?

She was looking at me as if she hadn't heard right.

Straight away I said: Course I can.

Three seconds later we were on the water. I mean, it must actually have been about an hour later. It was just that for the second time with Charlie I had that thing where I couldn't remember how I'd got somewhere. It was like in a film. Vwoom—and there you were. I just didn't get the chance to analyse it at the time. This bloody boat had a fair bit of horsepower. It shot across the Spree like a madman, and on the opposite bank was the concrete wall of some factory. I only just about managed to get it to turn. Instead of simply cutting the throttle like any non-idiotic person. We would've drowned on the spot, and there would've been fuck-all left of the boat. These boats really do go hell for leather the minute you start them up. No clutch or anything. I looked at Charlie. She didn't say a word. I reckon it nearly killed this boat guy we'd hired it from. I could see him just standing there on his jetty. How Charlie had managed to wheedle the boat out of him in the first place was a story in itself. Believe it or not, guys, I was actually really shy and stuff. I had inhibitions. And I personally would've bailed when I saw that Free German Youth boat hire place. The whole thing was dripping wet. There wasn't one single boat in the water. It was definitely off-season, after all, that close to Christmas. And the place was boarded up fit for World War Three. But Charlie found a hole in the fence and rang for the boat guy to come out of the shed and pleaded with him till he brought this boat out of the boathouse for us. I would never've thought it possible. I don't think the boat guy would either. I think Charlie could've done *anything* that day. She was unstoppable. She could've talked anyone into anything.

Out on the river she snuck under the cape with me. It was still raining like mad. A few degrees colder and we would've had the most beautiful snowstorm. None of you guys probably still remember last December. I'm sure it was pretty bloody damp in the boat, but I didn't even notice. Do you know what I mean, guys? Charlie laid her arm across the back of my seat and her head on my shoulder. It practically killed me. I was gradually starting to get the boat under control. I didn't know if there were traffic rules on the river—I remembered hearing about something along those lines. But that day there wasn't a single boat or steamer on the whole massive long Spree. I went to full throttle. The bow rose up in the air. It really wasn't bad, that boat. It was probably for the boat guy's private use. I started making loads of curves. Mostly to the left, because that pressed Charlie up against me. She didn't object at all. Then later on she took over the driving. At one point we narrowly missed a bridge pillar. Charlie didn't say a word. She still had pretty much the same expression on her face as when she'd come shooting out of her and Dieter's room.

Till then I'd never known that you can see a city from behind. Seeing Berlin from the Spree is like seeing it from behind. All those bloody great factory yards and warehouses.

At first I thought the rain was going to fill the boat. But it didn't. We must've been driving right out from underneath it. Although it didn't take long for us both to get soaked to the skin, even with the cape. Nothing could've kept out that rain. We were so wet we'd stopped caring ages ago. We might as well have gone swimming in our clothes. I don't know if you've ever had that, guys. When you're so wet that you really don't care about anything any more.

Eventually the warehouses stopped. Now it was all just country houses and stuff. Then we had to turn left or right at a fork in the river. Naturally I went left. I just hoped we'd be able to get back out of this lake we were in. By a different route, I mean. Wherever I went in my whole life I never wanted to go back the way I'd come. Not because I was superstitious or anything. It wasn't that. I just didn't want to. I found it boring, probably. I think that was another one of my obsessions. Like with the spray machine, for example. As we went whooshing past an island, Charlie started to get fidgety. She needed the loo. I sympathized. That's always the way when it rains. I looked for a gap in the reeds—luckily there were loads. More gaps than reeds, in fact. It was still absolutely chucking it down. We jumped onto the shore, and Charlie stealthed off somewhere. When she got back we huddled up under the cape in the soaking wet grass on this island. Or maybe it was just a peninsula. I never went back there. Then Charlie asked: Do you want to kiss me?

That killed me, guys. I started shaking. Charlie was still pissed off with Dieter, that was obvious. But I still kissed her. Her face smelt like laundry that had been bleached for a long time. Her mouth was icy cold, probably from all the rain. And then I just couldn't let go of her. She opened her eyes, but I just couldn't let go of her. It couldn't have gone any other way. She really was soaked to the skin, all down her legs and everything.

I read in some book once how a Negro, I mean an African man, comes to Europe and gets with his first white woman. He starts singing, some song from his homeland. I immediately zoned out. That may have been my biggest mistake—immediately zoning out from anything I hadn't experienced myself. With Charlie I genuinely could have started singing. I don't know if you've ever had that, guys. I was beyond help.

Then we went back to Berlin, the same way we'd come. Charlie didn't say anything, but she suddenly seemed to be in a big hurry. I didn't know why. I thought she must just be super-cold. I wanted her to come under the cape but she wouldn't, and she wouldn't say why. Even when I gave her the whole thing she wouldn't take it. The whole way back she didn't say a word. I was starting to feel like some kind of criminal. I started making curves again. I could see straight away that she was against it. She was just in such a hurry. Then we ran out of fuel. We paddled up to the next bridge. I wanted to go to the nearest petrol station and get some fuel while Charlie waited in the boat. But she got out. I couldn't stop her. She got out, ran up these dripping-wet metal steps, and was gone. I don't know why I didn't run after her. When I saw those bits in films and that where a girl's trying to leave and a guy's trying to stop her and she runs out the door and he just stands there in the doorway yelling after her, I always used to zone out. He only had to move about three steps and he would've caught up with her. And still I just sat there and let Charlie go. Two days later I was over the Jordan, and like an idiot I sat there and let her go and all I thought about was how I was going to have to take the boat back by myself. I don't know if any of you have ever thought about dying and that, guys. How one day you're just not there any more, no longer present, gone, departed, done for and expired, and never to return. For quite a while I used to think about it a lot, but I eventually gave up. I just couldn't imagine what it's s'posed to be like, in a coffin for example. All I could think of was stupid stuff. Like that I was lying in a coffin and it was completely dark and I got this horrendously itchy back, and I had to scratch it or I'd die. But it was so narrow that I couldn't move my arms. That's like being half dead already, guys, if you know what I mean. But it was still only suspended animation, not actual death. I just couldn't imagine that. Maybe people who can imagine it are already half dead—and I, being the idiot that I was, thought I was immortal. All I can tell you, guys, is never to think that. All I can tell you is never to think about a fucking boat or something and just sit there while someone you care about runs away from you.

Anyway, the boat guy was on the point of calling the river police when I eventually arrived back with the boat. But he was practically speechless with happiness that he'd got his tub back. I thought: this bloke isn't going to forget today either. At first I thought he was going to massively kick off about it. I put my dukes up. I was in just the right mood. I'd had such a go at the petrol pump attendant at the Sunday petrol station that he barely came out of it alive. He didn't want to fill up a jerrycan for me. He was one of these "And-who's-going-to-pay-for-the-can-if-we-never-see-it-again?" types. It's impossible to live with people like that.

Back at home I hung up my wet clothes on a nail. I didn't know what to do. I just *did not* know what to do. I was more down than I'd ever been. I put the Modern Soul boys on. I danced till I was boiling hot, for about two hours, but then I still didn't know what to do. I tried sleeping. I tossed and turned for about a million years on the bloody sofa. And when I woke up, World War Three had kicked off outside. A tank attack or something. I jumped off the bloody sofa and went to the door, and there was this beast with caterpillar tracks and steel plating coming right at me. A bulldozer. Hundred and fifty horsepower. I must've been yelling like an idiot. It came to a stop half a metre in front of me with the engine stalled. The bloke inside it, the driver, got down off his seat. Without warning he landed a straight right that sent me flying two metres through the air, back into my shack. I immediately did a backward roll. That's the quickest way to get back on your feet. I tucked in my chin for the counter-attack.

I would've hit him with a left hook that would've knocked him out. I don't think I mentioned that I was a proper left-hander. That was just about the only habit Mother Wibeau didn't manage to break me of. She tried everything, and like an idiot I went along with it. Until I developed a stutter and started wetting the bed. At that point the doctors called a halt. I was allowed to write with my left hand again, lost my stutter and stopped wetting the bed. The one good thing that came out of it was that later on I could do quite a lot with my right hand, much more than other people can with their left, for example. But my left hand was always stronger. Only this tank driver wasn't even thinking of putting his dukes up. Suddenly he went as white as a sheet and sat down on the ground. Then he said: Three seconds later and you would've been smashed to a pulp and I'd've been in the nick. And I've got three kids at home. Are you insane, still living here?

He was clearing the land with his scraper ready for the new builds. I probably looked like a bit of a lemon. I mumbled: A couple more days and I'll be out of here.

One thing had become clear to me during the night: that there was nothing left for me in Berlin any more. Without Charlie there was nothing left for me. That was what it came down to. True, she was the one that had initiated the whole kissing thing. But I was starting to realize that I'd still gone too far. As the man, I should've kept a clear head.

He said: Three more days. Till Christmas. Then your time's up, OK?!

He hoicked himself back up onto his tank. I had already been planning to finish the spray machine as quickly as possible, but three days was going to be tight. And I didn't want to skive off work. I didn't want to risk it all at the last moment by skiving. Zaremba would've turned up within twenty-four hours trying to sniff out what was going on. Or Addi. I was his most successfully reformed character, after all. I wanted to finish the spray machine, whack it down on the table in front of Addi and then skedaddle back to Mittenberg. Where I'd probably end up finishing my apprenticeship, for all I cared. That was the point I'd got to. I don't know if you get me, guys. I was probably just feeling weird because of Christmas. It's not like I was ever particularly into the whole Christmas malarkey. "O How Joyfully" and trees and cake and all that. But I was feeling weird for some reason. That's probably why I went *straight* to the post office to see if there was anything in my PO box from Willi. I never usually used to go till after work.

I got a funny feeling the moment I realized there was a special delivery letter from Willi in the PO box. I tore it open. It practically floored me. The key part was: You're probably going to kill me. But I couldn't take it any more. I told your mum where you are. So don't be surprised if she turns up. The letter had been sent two days ago. I knew what I had to do. I turned back straight away. If she'd taken the morning train from Mittenberg she would've been here already, walking times included. Which meant I still had a chance until the evening train. I bought an armful of milk cartons, because milk fills you up the quickest, and locked myself inside my shack. I closed all the curtains. And before I started I put up a note outside: Be right back!

Just in case. And it would do for the next stupid bulldozer as well, I thought. Then I lobbed myself at my spray machine. I started grafting like a madman, idiot that I was.

> "On Monday, the day before Christmas Eve, he didn't come to work. We weren't really that annoyed. It was unusually mild that day and we could have got a lot done, but we had already hit our annual target a long time before. And it was also the first time Edgar hadn't shown up for work since we'd brought him back on board."

That was just my luck, or whatever you want to call it. It was pretty much the only one of my calculations that turned out to be correct. Looking back, for example, I don't know why I was so certain about my spray machine. But I was—more certain than ever, in fact. The hydraulics idea was the most logical thing in the world. That mist you got when you were spraying was caused by compressed air. If you didn't use air, if you could apply the necessary pressure without it, then the whole thing would work. But the stupid thing was that now I didn't have time to make the nozzle I needed. I was going to have to wait till the brigade finished work, preferably till after it had gone dark, and nick Addi's one. Addi's spray machine had been written off—it was just lying there under our trailer. My next problem was generating the necessary horsepower for the two pressure cylinders. Luckily I'd actually managed to get hold of an electric motor with two horsepower. I even had to throttle it. I don't know if you can imagine what two horsepower can do when you give them free rein. You guys might be thinking the whole thing was just a bit of fun or something. A hobby. Bollocks. What Zaremba had said was true. That thing would have been a genuine sensation, technologically and economically. A bit like front-wheel drive in cars was back in the day, if you know what that is? Actually a step up from that, really. It would've made you famous, at least among the experts. I wanted to whack it down on the table in front of Addi and say: Press this little button here.

That really would've floored him, I reckon. Then I would've cleared things up with Charlie and then skedaddled. I mean, I obviously wouldn't *really* have whacked it down on the table. It was starting to get too big for that. It was starting to look like a bloody wind-powered sewage pump. I did have everything I needed, it was just that none of it fitted together properly. I *had* to start fudging it a bit. Otherwise I would never in my life have got it finished. What I needed most of all was an electric drill. And the motor obviously ran on three hundred and eighty volts. I reckoned it must have been out of an old lathe. So that meant I had to somehow step up the two hundred and twenty volts in the shack. I just hoped the transformer I had was working. I didn't have any kind of voltmeter. That was probably another nail in my coffin. And I definitely didn't have time to go looking for one. Anyway, you don't find voltmeters just lying about the place the way you might find a couple of old truck shock absorbers. Which you also didn't exactly find lying around, to be fair, and which weren't necessarily old, either, but you could get your hands on them if you wanted to. Without the shock absorbers I would've been screwed. Though the casings could've done with being thicker, for that amount of pressure. Which made me think I might need to widen the opening of the nozzle. It would've made the jet thicker, but I wanted to start off with oil-based paint anyway. By about twelve I was at the point where I needed to go and get the nozzle so I could adjust it. I slunk off in the direction of the building site. I wasn't under the illusion that I was already finished and that it was going to work straight away on the first attempt. But the way things stood I still had all night to make improvements. I was a bit more chilled now. The earliest Mother Wiebau could arrive was the next morning. She'd given me another chance. On site everything was in darkness. I dived under our trailer and started loosening the cap nut. The stupid thing was, the only multi-purpose tool I had was this shitty pipe wrench. And the nut was tight as fuck. I nearly bust my balls trying to loosen it. At that moment I heard Zaremba in the trailer, with a woman. Like I mentioned earlier. I'd probably interrupted them. At any rate, when I crawled out from under the trailer he was standing there in front of me. He growled: Ey?

He was standing right in front of me, staring at me. Though he did have the light from the trailer in his eyes. He had our brigade's little axe in his hand. At the time I assumed he was just blinded by the light. But he had this smile in his little pig-eyes. At *that* distance he must've been able to see me. I didn't move. My only advice in a situation like that is just not to move, guys. I reckon Zaremba was the last person ever to see me, and I reckon he knew exactly what was going on, as well.

The whole way back I didn't see a bloody soul. You might as well have been in Mittenberg at that time of night. After eight p.m. Berlin looked exactly like Mittenberg. Everyone was sat in front of the TV. Apart from a few teenagers who snuck into parks or cinemas, or who were into sport and were out training. Not a bloody soul on the streets.

By about two I had the nozzle connected. I poured half the oil paint into the cartridge. Then I checked the wiring again. I had another look over the whole thing. I think I already mentioned what it looked like. It wasn't technically acceptable, by normal standards. But it was the concept I was interested in. That was probably the last thought I had before I pressed the button. I was that much of an idiot I had actually taken the doorbell button off the outside of the shack. I could've used any normal switch. But I'd taken off the doorbell button, just so I could say to Addi: Press this button here.

Maybe I was an idiot, guys. The last thing I was aware of was that it was very light and that my hand wouldn't come off the button. That was all I was aware of. It must have been that the whole hydraulic system didn't move. That must have sent the voltage up massively high so that when you put your hand on it, it wouldn't come off. That was it. Take it easy, guys!

"When Edgar didn't show up again on the Tuesday we went to look for him, around noon.

The police were at the property. When we said who we were they told us what had happened. And that there was no point in going to the hospital. We were in complete shock. Then they let us into the summer house. The first thing I noticed was that the walls were covered in oil paint, particularly in the kitchen. It was still wet. It was the same paint we'd been using for kitchen panelling. The whole place smelt of paint and charred insulation material. The kitchen table was on its side. All the glass was shattered. On the floor there was a charred electric motor, bent pipe ends, bits of garden hose. We told the officers what we knew, but we didn't have an explanation for it any more than they did. Then Zaremba told them which factory Edgar had come from. And that was the end of it.

We didn't do any more work that day. I sent everyone home. Only Zaremba didn't go. He started dragging our old spray machine out from under the trailer. He examined it, and then he showed me that the nozzle was missing. We went back to Edgar's summer house straight away. We found the nozzle in the kitchen inside an old piece of gas pipe. I gathered up everything else that was lying around, even the smallest bits, and the things that were screwed onto the table. When I got home I cleaned off the paint. Over Christmas I tried to figure out how it had all fitted together. Like an incredibly complex jigsaw puzzle. I couldn't manage it. Half the components were probably still missing—especially a pressure tank or something of that sort. I wanted to go back into the summer house, but it had already been knocked down."

It was probably for the best. I wouldn't have survived the failure of the spray machine anyway. At least, I was almost at the point where I could understand Old Werther when he said he couldn't go on any more. I mean, I would never in my life have given up the ghost voluntarily. Hung myself from the nearest peg or anything. Never. But I never *really* would've gone back to Mittenberg. I don't know if you get me. That may've been my biggest mistake: my whole life I could never admit defeat. I just couldn't swallow it. I was that much of an idiot, I always wanted to win.

"But still. I can't stop thinking about Edgar's machine. I can't help feeling that he was onto something sensational, the kind of thing you don't come up with every day. More than just an obsession, anyway. No doubt about it."

"And the pictures?! Do you think there might still be any of them around anywhere?"

"The pictures?—We'd forgotten about them.

They were covered in paint. They were probably destroyed along with the building."

"Can you describe any of them?"

"I don't know anything about art. I'm just an ordinary house painter. But Zaremba reckoned they were pretty good. No wonder, with you as a father."

"I'm not a painter. I never have been a painter. I'm a structural engineer. I haven't seen Edgar since he was five. I know nothing about him—even now. Charlie, a summer house that's been knocked down, pictures that have been destroyed, and this machine."

"I can't tell you any more than that. But we shouldn't have left him to muddle through on his own. I don't know where he went wrong. The doctors said it was something to do with electricity."

Pushkin Press

Pushkin Press was founded in 1997, and publishes novels, essays, memoirs, children's books—everything from timeless classics to the urgent and contemporary.

Our books represent exciting, high-quality writing from around the world: we publish some of the twentieth century's most widely acclaimed, brilliant authors such as Stefan Zweig, Marcel Aymé, Teffi, Antal Szerb, Gaito Gazdanov and Yasushi Inoue, as well as compelling and award-winning contemporary writers, including Andrés Neuman, Edith Pearlman, Eka Kurniawan, Ayelet Gundar-Goshen and Chigozie Obioma.

Pushkin Press publishes the world's best stories, to be read and read again. To discover more, visit www.pushkinpress.com.

THE SPECTRE OF ALEXANDER WOLF

GAITO GAZDANOV

'A mesmerising work of literature' Antony Beevor

SUMMER BEFORE THE DARK

VOLKER WEIDERMANN

'For such a slim book to convey with such poignancy the extinction of a generation of "Great Europeans" is a triumph' *Sunday Telegraph*

MESSAGES FROM A LOST WORLD

STEFAN ZWEIG

'At a time of monetary crisis and political disorder… Zweig's celebration of the brotherhood of peoples reminds us that there is another way' *The Nation*

THE EVENINGS

GERARD REVE

'Not only a masterpiece but a cornerstone manqué of modern European literature' Tim Parks, *Guardian*

BINOCULAR VISION

EDITH PEARLMAN

'A genius of the short story' Mark Lawson, *Guardian*

IN THE BEGINNING WAS THE SEA

TOMÁS GONZÁLEZ

'Smoothly intriguing narrative, with its touches of sinister, Patricia Highsmith-like menace' *Irish Times*

BEWARE OF PITY

STEFAN ZWEIG

'Zweig's fictional masterpiece' *Guardian*

THE ENCOUNTER

PETRU POPESCU

'A book that suggests new ways of looking at the world and our place within it' *Sunday Telegraph*

WAKE UP, SIR!

JONATHAN AMES

'The novel is extremely funny but it is also sad and poignant, and almost incredibly clever' *Guardian*

THE WORLD OF YESTERDAY

STEFAN ZWEIG

'*The World of Yesterday* is one of the greatest memoirs of the twentieth century, as perfect in its evocation of the world Zweig loved, as it is in its portrayal of how that world was destroyed' David Hare

WAKING LIONS

AYELET GUNDAR-GOSHEN

'A literary thriller that is used as a vehicle to explore big moral issues. I loved everything about it' *Daily Mail*

FOR A LITTLE WHILE

RICK BASS

'Bass is, hands down, a master of the short form, creating in a few pages a natural world of mythic proportions' *New York Times Book Review*

JOURNEY BY MOONLIGHT

ANTAL SZERB

'Just divine… makes you imagine the author has had private access to your own soul' Nicholas Lezard, *Guardian*

BEFORE THE FEAST

SAŠA STANIŠIĆ

'Exceptional… cleverly done, and so mesmerising from the off… thought-provoking and energetic' *Big Issue*

A SIMPLE STORY

LEILA GUERRIERO

'An epic of noble proportions… [Guerriero] is a mistress of the telling phrase or the revealing detail' *Spectator*

FORTUNES OF FRANCE

ROBERT MERLE

1 *The Brethren*

2 *City of Wisdom and Blood*

3 *Heretic Dawn*

'Swashbuckling historical fiction' *Guardian*

TRAVELLER OF THE CENTURY

ANDRÉS NEUMAN

'A beautiful, accomplished novel: as ambitious as it is generous, as moving as it is smart' Juan Gabriel Vásquez, *Guardian*

A WORLD GONE MAD

ASTRID LINDGREN

'A remarkable portrait of domestic life in a country maintaining a fragile peace while war raged all around' *New Statesman*

MIRROR, SHOULDER, SIGNAL

DORTHE NORS

'Dorthe Nors is fantastic!' Junot Díaz

RED LOVE: THE STORY OF AN EAST GERMAN FAMILY

MAXIM LEO

'Beautiful and supremely touching… an unbearably poignant description of a world that no longer exists' *Sunday Telegraph*

THE BEAUTIFUL BUREAUCRAT

HELEN PHILLIPS

'Funny, sad, scary and beautiful. I love it' Ursula K. Le Guin

THE RABBIT BACK LITERATURE SOCIETY

PASI ILMARI JÄÄSKELÄINEN

'Wonderfully knotty… a very grown-up fantasy masquerading as quirky fable. Unexpected, thrilling and absurd' *Sunday Telegraph*

BEAUTY IS A WOUND

EKA KURNIAWAN

'An unforgettable all-encompassing epic' *Publishers Weekly*

BARCELONA SHADOWS

MARC PASTOR

'As gruesome as it is gripping… the writing is extraordinarily vivid… Highly recommended' *Independent*

MEMORIES—FROM MOSCOW TO THE BLACK SEA

TEFFI

'Wonderfully idiosyncratic, coolly heartfelt and memorable' William Boyd, *Sunday Times*

WHILE THE GODS WERE SLEEPING

ERWIN MORTIER

'A monumental, phenomenal book' *De Morgen*

BUTTERFLIES IN NOVEMBER

AUÐUR AVA ÓLAFSDÓTTIR

'A funny, moving and occasionally bizarre exploration of life's upheavals and reversals' *Financial Times*

BY BLOOD

ELLEN ULLMAN

'Delicious and intriguing' *Daily Telegraph*

THE LAST DAYS

LAURENT SEKSIK

'Mesmerising… Seksik's portrait of Zweig's final months is dignified and tender' *Financial Times*